e
413

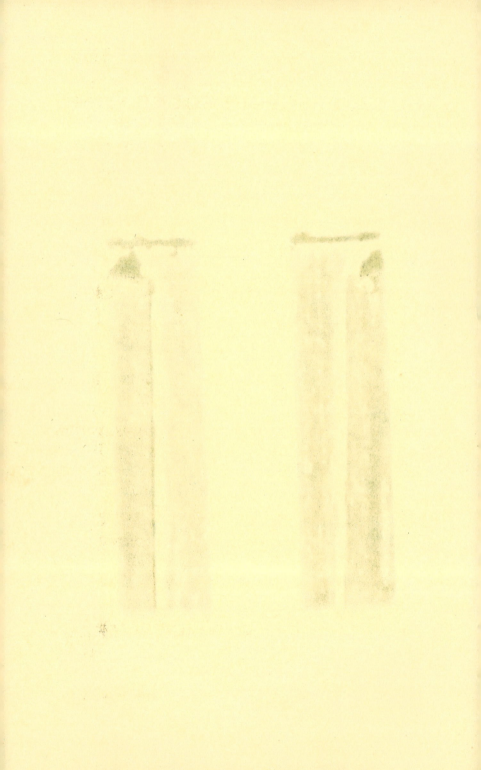

I've travelled the world twice over,
Met the famous: saints and sinners,
Poets and artists, kings and queens,
Old stars and hopeful beginners,
I've been where no-one's been before,
Learned secrets from writers and cooks
All with one library ticket
To the wonderful world of books.

© JANICE JAMES.

A HAVEN OF DANGER

Detective Chief Inspector Tansey found himself personally involved in his latest case when a friend went to live in a select retirement home, run by caring Dr Cassidy and his delightful family. Sadly, Evenlode House soon proved far from the haven it had promised to be. Petty theft was followed by an outbreak of food poisoning, then murder and attempted murder, and finally arson and another death. Who was to blame? Who, apart from the local reporter, had it in for Evenlode House? And why?

JOHN PENN

A HAVEN
OF DANGER

Complete and Unabridged

ULVERSCROFT
Leicester

First published in Great Britain in 1993 by
HarperCollins Publishers
London

First Large Print Edition
published December 1994
by arrangement with
HarperCollins Publishers
London

British Library CIP Data

Penn, John
A haven of danger.—Large print ed.—
Ulverscroft large print series: mystery
I. Title
823.914 [F]

ISBN 0–7089–3207–X

Published by
F. A. Thorpe (Publishing) Ltd.
Anstey, Leicestershire
Set by Words & Graphics Ltd.
Anstey, Leicestershire
Printed and bound in Great Britain by
T. J. Press (Padstow) Ltd., Padstow, Cornwall

This book is printed on acid-free paper

The First Letter

Evenlode House,
Evenlode,
Oxfordshire,
May 25th 199-

M<small>Y</small> dear Dick,
Forgive me for not writing to you before, but packing up the house where John and I had been so happy for so many years was a traumatic experience. In addition to the physical effort it required — not inconsiderable, in spite of all the help I had — there were innumerable decisions to be made. Some were obviously important, even vital, others of no real significance. It was these small matters which seemed to cause me most concern and a surprising amount of heartache. For example, what was I to do with a little marble bowl that we had bought in Pisa. Intending it for flowers, we discovered on reaching home that it wouldn't hold water. Of

1

course we should have thrown it away at once, but somehow we didn't. And now it reminded me of our honeymoon in Italy — the first of so many visits to a country that John loved almost as much as his own. I have to admit that it cost me to put that silly little bowl in the rubbish skip.

But enough of feeling sorry for myself. I'm well aware that I'm a fortunate woman. I had a wonderful marriage for fifty years and, though John and I had our sorrows — as when Tim was killed in that accident — we also had many blessings, more than our fair share, I sometimes thought. What's more, I'm still lucky. At seventy-four I have excellent health apart from a few twinges of arthritis, and, thanks to my dear John, no money worries. I'm looking forward to a comfortable and not uninteresting old age.

You'll be glad to hear that I'm sure I made the right decision in coming to Evenlode. I have no regrets about giving up the house. It was much too big for one old woman, and it had too many ghosts. Even happy ghosts aren't really a *good idea. They add to one's solitude.*

Evenlode is the perfect answer for me and for those like me — elderly people with no close relations willing and able to be responsible for them, people who seek security and comfort and privacy without isolation. For such as us it's an absolute haven. This is partly due to the set-up. Everyone has his or her own separate apartment, but there are delightful public rooms and, while the place is run like an efficient luxury hotel or a superior London club, the atmosphere can only be described as homelike.

This is due to the family who have created Evenlode, chiefly Dr and Mrs Cassidy, but also the younger members of their family. They all take a personal interest in us, without being nosey. As to the residents themselves, though the Cassidys would express horror at the suggestion, I suspect that we are chosen with care, or at least put off if not thought desirable. Be that as it may, we are a surprisingly compatible collection, which certainly helps.

Anyway, Dick, after reading this long screed you'll know that I'm as happy here as I could be anywhere without John. I hope you'll come and see me some weekend. There are guest rooms.

Meanwhile, my love to you and Hilary and little Peter.

Your affectionate aunt,
Anne,

This letter from Mrs Anne Horne was addressed to Detective Chief Inspector Richard Tansey at his home near Kidlington outside Oxford.

1

HUGH CASSIDY woke instantly as his alarm sounded. Long years as a practising doctor had taught him to pass from deep sleep to full wakefulness in seconds and, though the need was no longer so urgent, he still found it a useful ability. Now he sat up at once, ran a hand through his thick dark hair, untinged by grey though he was in his middle fifties, and swung his long legs out of bed.

"Wake up, Cindy," he said. "Alarm's gone."

Lucinda Cassidy groaned. She was a pretty, plump woman with an enviable peaches and cream complexion that her daughter Jill had inherited. Jill sometimes thought how lucky she had been to have taken after her mother, and not inherited her father's craggy features as her brother had done. But she loved and admired both her parents, as indeed did Simon. The Cassidys were a close-knit family.

5

"It's going to be a busy day," Hugh said, making for the adjoining bathroom.

"When isn't it?" said Lucinda.

She spoke without animosity. She wouldn't have changed her present way of life for any other, in spite of the fact that she was working harder and with more responsibility than when she had been a nurse. She was happy. Why shouldn't she be? She and Hugh had achieved — were achieving — an ambition for which they had scarcely dared to hope.

Hugh had been a good, conscientious GP, and Lucinda had been an efficient, caring nurse, but they had both come to dislike the red tape and restrictions of the national health system. They dreamt of getting out, perhaps of starting a private nursing home, but accepted that this could be only a dream. Then changing circumstances made them believe that the dream was conceivably realizable.

Simon, who had always refused to consider medicine as a career and had decided to become a hotelier, brought home for a weekend a fellow-trainee with whom he had become friendly. This was Patrick Donne, a Dubliner,

6

with all the charm of the Irish. He and Jill Cassidy were immediately attracted to each other, and within the year they were married. Thankfully Jill gave up nursing, which she had never liked, and became a receptionist in the hotel where Patrick and Simon worked.

Three months later Patrick's father died, leaving him a modest inheritance. At the same time Evenlode House came on to the market. It had been designed as an exclusive country hotel, but the company responsible for building it had gone into liquidation, and it was now for sale at a bargain price. The temptation was too much for the Cassidys. They saw it as the potential fulfilment of all their dreams.

Of course, even as a bargain, the price was high and the risks great. Nevertheless, the Cassidys knew they would never forgive themselves if they didn't take the chance. They got together what money they could of their own, all their savings, Patrick's inheritance and a couple of thousand — the proverbial drop in the bucket — from Sarah Field; Sarah, an old school friend of Jill's, with no family of her own, had more or less adopted the Cassidys and was determined to have a share in Evenlode. After that they had prepared a competent business plan and taken out an enormous mortgage. They were on their way.

They had clear ideas about what they intended. Evenlode was not to be a residential hotel or a nursing home, but a place where elderly, reasonably healthy people could own their own apartments and be able to live a pleasant, secure and comfortable life, free from all domestic worries, with common facilities such as a heated swimming pool and spacious grounds, with as much or as little privacy as they wished and with medical skills at immediate hand. It wouldn't come cheap. And Cassidy's lawyer complained that his hair had gone two shades greyer working out the details — but that was a couple of years ago and, though inevitably there had been difficulties and problems, Evenlode was now prospering.

"I thought Patrick and I might check the supplies today," Hugh said, returning from the bathroom. "It's almost the end where around."

...inda shook her head. "What a ...I've never known anyone like him ...osing things, or rather mislaying ... It's difficult to imagine him as ...n-powered businessman, running a ... industrial concern, but that's what ...s."

... had a host of secretaries to look ...him then," Patrick said.

...d a wife!" said Jill, removing ...k's plate. "Breakfast is over!" she ...ed.

* * *

...n Cassidy, a younger version of ...ther, was equally competent. On ...g in Oxford he dealt first with the ...and, with that safely locked in the ...of his car, he bought the cosmetics ...after some trouble matching it, ...'s embroidery silk.

...was coming out of the needlework ...that he almost bumped into Ashley ...nde, whose private estate bordered ...at of the Cassidys. A man in ...rly sixties, with a crest of white

of the month and the wine stock's getting very low. We really must keep a better cellar, Cindy."

"Yes, we must. I didn't realize our oldies would get through so much. They certainly do themselves proud. Still, why not?"

"Why not indeed?" Hugh laughed. "Not for us to grudge them. It's a question of knowing their tastes — and learning from what they have to say. Mr Barnard's quite an expert on wine."

"Well, if there's any particular shortfall before the next delivery, remember Simon's going into Oxford this morning."

"Right."

Hugh, already dressed, was putting on his watch and checking the contents of his pockets. Lucinda was on her way to the bathroom. Their day had begun. The time was six twenty-two.

Shortly afterwards they met in the kitchen, where they were joined by the Donnes and Simon and Sarah. Here, over breakfast, the family discussed any problems they faced or could foresee. This was the one time of each day they had to themselves. None of the staff slept in the house. The two women from the nearby village who helped with the cleaning didn't come till eight. The assistant cook, a waiter and the gardener arrived even later. Except by special arrangement, which only a few chose to make, the residents had continental breakfasts in their apartments.

"What decision have we reached about the duckling?" Jill asked as her mother stood up and started to clear the table. "I promised I'd let old Compton know if we wanted them."

"We'll have them, Jill. They're a fair price," said Lucinda.

"And it's a good thing to keep in with the local farmers," Hugh added. "Besides, roast duck! Lovely." He sniffed loudly as if savouring the aroma.

"Don't count your ducklings, Dad." Patrick was sardonic. "There may not be enough for everyone, and family comes last in this establishment."

"Not always," Lucinda protested.

Hugh laughed. "There's one wine I know we need without checking, Simon. Chablis. The usual. At least three cases. You won't forget?"

"I won't. Any more commis I'm in Oxford?"

Both Sarah and Jill wanted and when Simon suggested buy them as easily in Colo assured him he was wrong. wanted some embroidery sill off to find a sample. Lucinda might look for any 'interesti the market.

"Perhaps I shouldn't h Simon said. "I'll hardly h do all this before I get to — which is the main reaso at all."

"The wine's the most — except for your dentist, said Patrick, who was still e the table was by now almo

"And my silk." Sarah dro of scarlet silk in front of Sin up a spectacle case. "Lo found. Mr Poynter's lost sp have left them on the desk into the office yesterday af

"You didn't find his w you?" Hugh inquired.

"No, but it'll turn up

10

11

hair, a red face and rather bulbous eyes, Ormonde carried himself with the exaggerated straight back of a sergeant-major on parade. He was said to be seriously rich, but he was not a good neighbour. He was always complaining — usually without just cause.

"Hello, Cassidy," he greeted Simon. "Don't tell me you've taken up knitting."

"No, sir. I'm saving that for my old age."

Ormonde nodded in acceptance of the remark, but didn't smile. "Lucky to have met you," he said. "You've saved me another phone call to your father. He's still done nothing about that damned elm tree of yours. The next storm we have it'll come down on my property, mark my words, and when it does it'll ruin my drystone wall. That'll cost you a pretty penny to put to rights again."

"I'll give him your message, sir," Simon said coldly.

"You do that!"

With another brusque nod Ashley Ormonde moved off with his companion, whom Simon had recognized as one of his buddies, a man called John Rayner, a

13

property developer. Rayner had taken no part in the conversation, but had stood by, smiling superciliously.

Simon glared after them. The elm tree was a perpetual cause of contention between Ormonde and the Cassidys, but Simon had inspected it with his father and their gardener the previous day. Granted that elms didn't have the most secure of roots, the tree had no sign of disease, and they could see no justification for applying for permission to cut it down. Even if it were to be blown down in a storm the chance that it would fall on to Ormonde's property, as he asserted, was no more than evens. They had decided that he was merely being unpleasant, and no action was necessary, but it was clear that he didn't intend to let the matter lie.

Seething with anger, Simon treated himself to a cup of coffee, collected his car and drove to North Oxford. His dentist's surgery was in a side street off the Banbury Road. It was a busy street and it wasn't always easy to find a parking place, but today Simon was lucky and found himself able to park almost opposite the house in an ample space.

Forty minutes later when he left the dentist's the space had shrunk. The car that had previously been behind him had gone, and been replaced by an old Ford. Except to register that it had left him little room to get clear he scarcely noticed it. And he paid no attention whatsoever to the girl in the very short summer dress who, carrying a raincoat and an oversized weekend bag, was about to cross the street. He got into his car, started the engine, and thought about getting back to Evenlode. Automatically he backed a trifle in order to manoeuvre out of his parking space, and was at once aware of a fist banging on the window beside him.

Startled, Simon stalled the engine. The fist continued to bang while, with the other hand, the man seemed to be pointing to the rear of the car. At least Simon presumed it was a man; in jeans and a sweatshirt, with a crash helmet obscuring the face, the person could have been either male or female. Simon turned and looked behind him, but could see no reason for the agitation. He wound down the window.

"What's the matter?"

"The girl!" It was a man's voice. "You'll kill her!"

"What girl?"

But the man had stepped away from the window, though he still pointed to the back of the car. Simon got out and went around, not knowing what he expected to see.

"Oh God!" he said.

The girl who lay crumpled on the ground between the rear bumper of Simon's car and the front bumper of the Ford that had parked behind him, looked up and tried to smile as she smoothed down her dress. She was a pretty girl with short curly fair hair and wide blue eyes. But she was very pale. There was a smear of blood on her cheek and more blood on her dress. Simon was horrified.

"I'm sorry," he said, "terribly sorry."

"It was my fault. I thought I could pass behind you. I didn't realize you were going to back."

"I should have looked, been more

careful," Simon reproached himself. "Are you badly hurt? Do you want an ambulance?" Simon looked about him in search of help, but the man with the crash helmet had disappeared, and no other passer-by seemed to be taking the least interest in them.

"No, no. Let me try to stand up. I don't think there's anything broken. But I've cut my leg." This time she managed to smile, but she winced as Simon helped her to her feet. There was a long scratch down one leg. She leant against him. "Sorry. I feel a bit dizzy," she said.

"Come and sit in the car."

"Thank you." She let Simon lead her to the front of the car and help her into the seat. She had found a handkerchief and started to mop rather ineffectually at her leg. "My bag, please. Could you fetch it?"

"Of course."

Simon collected the bag and came to sit beside the girl. It was obvious that she wasn't seriously hurt, but she was in some pain, and it was his fault, his carelessness. If she'd been a bitch she could have created a hell of a fuss, but

17

she hadn't. She wasn't even blaming him. He wished he knew what he should do.

"Would you like me to drive you to a hospital — that leg should be looked at, though I don't think it's very deep. Or even a doctor? Or would you rather I drove you home?"

She shook her head. "No hospital. No doctors. Really. I'm all right. It's only a scratch, but it's bled rather a lot."

"Then I'll take you home."

"No. You can't. Just give me five minutes and I'll be OK."

"Why can't I take you home?" Simon persisted.

"Because I don't have a home!" The girl sounded exasperated. "Look, it's none of your business, but . . . My mother died a short while ago and I planned to come to Oxford to stay with a girlfriend and find a job, but when I got here this morning I discovered she had a — a living-in partner, and I wasn't wanted. So there you are. Heaven knows why I'm burdening you with my sordid little story but you did ask for it."

"You mean you've nowhere to go?"

"That's right. But I'll find somewhere

and get a job. I've a bit of money to tide me over."

Simon regarded her doubtfully but he knew he couldn't just dump her and her bag on the pavement and drive away, not after he had hurt her. If it hadn't been for that character banging on the window he might have killed her.

"You'd better come home with me," he said.

"Oh no! No, thank you!" She laughed and started to get out of the car.

Simon flushed; it was obvious what she was thinking. "I live with my parents," he said, "and my sister and her husband — and for that matter a host of other people. My father's a doctor and my mother was a nurse," he added.

"What do you mean?" the girl asked, but she had let go of the door handle and when Simon explained she said, "That would be very kind, but won't your family object to having a strange girl thrust on them?"

"Not if I can introduce her by name," Simon said.

The girl laughed, showing small white even teeth. "My name's Valerie Rowan.

Val to my friends."

"I'm Simon Cassidy, and only my enemies shorten my first name."

"I'll try not to become one of those." She glanced down at the floor. "Simon, I'm sorry, but I'm beginning to bleed again. Can I have your handkerchief? Mine's not much use."

"Yes, of course — and the sooner we get home so that Dad can look at your leg the better."

Simon gave her his handkerchief, though with slight reluctance. It was one of fine cambric with his initials embroidered in a corner. Sarah, who was an expert needle-woman had given him half a dozen on his last birthday. He could only hope that Val's blood would wash out.

"Let's go," he said, starting the engine. "You can tell me about yourself on the way, Val. What sort of job did you hope to get in Oxford? Have you lots of qualifications?"

"None, Simon, if you mean degrees or certificates or things like that. I've a few O-levels. That's all. I had to leave school when Mother was taken ill. There was no one else to look after her. My father walked out when I was a kid. I hardly remember him. But I can cook — no fancy stuff — and clean, and I know a certain amount about nursing; I had to learn to look after Mother. I was hoping I might get a job as a mother's help, perhaps."

"That sounds reasonable," said Simon. He spoke absent-mindedly. He appeared to be concentrating on the traffic, but he was wondering if there might not be work for Val Rowan at Evenlode House.

2

MRS ANNE HORNE was sitting in the drawing-room of Evenlode House shortly before lunch a week after Simon's visit to Oxford. A big, heavy woman whose arthritis bothered her more than she had admitted in her letter to Dick Tansey, Anne was a kind and cheerful character. Not gregarious by nature, she nevertheless enjoyed spending a little of each day being sociable, which usually meant having a preprandial drink, when she was often joined by three or four of the other residents with whom she had become friendly.

Today she was early. She had nodded a good morning to a small group gathered in front of an open french window, but hadn't joined them. Inevitably in any club or residential hotel, any office or staff room — or for that matter any large family — an individual will find some of his or her fellows more congenial than others; couples pair off and coteries

22

are formed. Evenlode was no exception. Nor did the Cassidys object, though, as the leaseholds on the apartments were sold and the residents settled down, they watched to make sure that no one was unwillingly excluded.

There had never been any likelihood that this would happen to Mrs Horne. To begin with she had been wary, knowing that it would be wiser to make friends slowly rather than to have to detach herself from those with whom fuller acquaintance might prove she had little in common. But before long she was drawn into a loosely-knit circle whose company she enjoyed and who never trespassed on her privacy. Among them was Morag Luton.

"Hello, Anne. Isn't it chilly for June?"

Mrs Luton had come into the drawing-room and sat down beside Anne. In appearance they were opposites. Morag was small and dark, with pointed features and quick unexpected movements, reminding Anne of a sparrow. She looked frail, but was in fact in excellent health. She did, however, feel the cold, having spent much of her adult life in the Far East.

"You should borrow some of my surplus fat," Anne said.

"Better still, try a whisky, Morag." Kenneth Barnard had joined them. His deep, rather fruity voice carried to the bar, where Patrick was arranging glasses. Patrick hid a smile. He didn't hear Morag's reply, but he had no need; he knew that Mrs Luton would say that she never drank whisky, and Kenneth would then argue that it was better for her than gin. Idly Patrick wondered if, when he and Jill were in their seventies, they would repeat themselves so often, and tell the same stories over and over again. But there was no malice in his reflections; he liked the oldies, some more than others, and the six-foot Kenneth Barnard, who had once got a Rugby blue at Cambridge, was one of his favourites.

"Our usuals, Patrick," Barnard boomed towards the small bar at the end of the room.

"Coming right up, sir," said Patrick, who liked to play the part of barman.

He served them, then wrote the drinks on their three separate accounts. It was one of the few rules at Evenlode that all orders from the bar were charged to individuals — private entertaining took place in apartments — and it was a sensible rule which prevented polite arguments over who should pay. It had another advantage. Hugh Cassidy had insisted from the beginning that the mark-up on drinks in the bar should be kept to a minimum, and this encouraged residents to socialize; the Cassidys were well aware the rich appreciated bargains as much as those less well off.

"Wait a week or two, Morag," Kenneth Barnard advised as she again complained about the weather. "Then go and visit your nephew in Canada. You say he's always asking you. Ottawa in July and August should suit you. It'll be nice and hot and steamy."

"But that will be vacation time, and Angus won't be there. He usually takes a summer course at some other university, or he goes on a lecture tour." Morag was proud of her nephew, the only child of her late husband's brother who had been part of the brain-drain to North America in the late 'forties. "He's a very clever man."

"He must be," Barnard agreed pleasantly.

"Do you know Canada well, Kenneth?" Anne asked, thinking that Kenneth Barnard's definition of 'a very clever man' probably differed from Morag Luton's.

"Not well, no. We used to go up there occasionally when we lived in New York, mostly on business. But, as you know, I'm not an academic."

Anne smiled. In fact, she did not know. Unlike some of the other residents Kenneth Barnard did not talk much of his past. He was a reticent man, who spoke vaguely of business that seemed to have taken him around the world many times. Anne, who in her quiet way was an intelligent woman, suspected that he had worked for the Government, and that his 'business' had been connected with defence, but she wouldn't have dreamt of asking him. She had noticed that he had a happy facility for turning aside direct questions.

"And who have we here?" Barnard said as Valerie Rowan approached them. "A pretty young girl, bringing news of the culinary delights in store for us today."

Val flushed. Mr Barnard disconcerted her; she wasn't sure how to react to his remarks. "It's just a copy of the menu, sir, if you'd be interested to see it in advance."

"I'm always interested in food," Barnard said, taking the menu from her and passing it to Anne, "and Mrs Cassidy always does us proud."

"Are you going to stay on at Evenlode, Val?" Morag asked kindly as the girl turned to go.

"I'm not sure, Mrs Luton. For a while, I expect."

In fact, Lucinda Cassidy had spoken to Val that morning and asked her if she would like to stay. In the first couple of days after Simon had brought her to Evenlode Val had been treated as a guest, but then, without being asked, she had begun to help, doing any odd job that came up, and she had proved herself useful. Now, Lucinda had suggested that this should be put on a more formal basis, which meant that Val should provide a character reference and, as she had never been employed before, make the necessary arrangements with the Social Security and other authorities in Oxford. Hugh would know, Lucinda said. She also explained that they could only offer board and lodging and a very small wage, but there would be no commitment on Val's part; she could look for better paid, possibly more congenial work, and leave whenever was convenient to her.

It was a generous offer, which had caused some controversy in the family. Hugh Cassidy had argued that they didn't need extra help, and anyhow they couldn't afford it. Jill and Sarah had agreed with him, but Lucinda had pointed out that the arrangement was merely temporary and, because of the accident, they did owe Val something. To no one's surprise, Simon had vehemently supported his mother and Patrick, who knew how attracted to Val Simon was, had sided with them. In the end Hugh had yielded, to Val's relief when Simon told her about the argument.

"I hope she stays," Morag said when Val had gone. "Another young face around the place is always welcome."

"I'm not so sure everyone would agree

with you," said Kenneth.

"What do you mean? Why not?"

"Ah!" he said; sometimes he could be irritating.

Anne said, "I imagine Kenneth is referring to Sarah. Sarah doesn't make much of a secret of her feelings for Simon, and she wouldn't be human if she didn't feel a bit jealous of Val. Simon's obviously very taken with the girl."

"Yes, I suppose so." The idea didn't seem to have occurred to Morag.

Their gossip was interrupted by the arrival of Melissa Sarson, who strode purposefully into the room, nodded at Patrick to bring her usual pre-luncheon drink and accepted the chair that Kenneth Barnard drew out for her. On her arrival at Evenlode House Melissa, Lady Sarson's flamboyant personality had0 caused something of a stir, but this had passed.

Except perhaps for an amused smile or a whispered sardonic remark, Lady Sarson now created no more interest than the plain dowdy Miss Dorothy Webb, who had arrived at Evenlode on the same day. But Melissa was a striking woman.

Tall and thin, with a ravaged face, heavy make-up and an imperious manner, she tended to favour trouser suits or colourful caftans and large jewellery which might or might not have been genuine. Patrick, who admired her greatly, believed that it was.

He brought the White Lady that she habitually drank before lunch and put it on the table beside her. As a rule she would give him a broad smile of thanks, but today she didn't notice him, and this caused him to linger momentarily in expectation of some acknowledgement. Only when he saw Kenneth Barnard shake his head as if to silence her did it occur to him that he might have appeared to be listening to their conversation.

Angry at the implication, Patrick returned to the bar. He had not been eavesdropping. But he *had* heard part of what Lady Sarson had been saying, and he couldn't help wondering what she had been talking about. Involuntarily he recalled her words.

" . . . I'm absolutely positive, and so is Dorothy. She's still very upset about it. It's really a most unpleasant thing to have happen in a place like Evenlode . . . "

As the gong sounded for lunch he told himself to forget the incident, but this proved to be impossible, and indeed he kept on recalling it throughout the day.

★ ★ ★

The mystery was solved that evening.

After dinner Kenneth Barnard asked if he and Lady Sarson might have a word privately with Dr and Mrs Cassidy. There was no question of refusing, though the request was unusual. One or other of the senior Cassidys was always available during the day, and a member of the family remained on duty in the evening, but it was accepted that unless some urgent matter arose Dr and Mrs Cassidy should not be disturbed after dinner.

Hugh asked the two residents to come to the office and, once the four of them were seated, Barnard apologized to the Cassidys for intruding on them at such a time.

"To tell you the truth," he said, "we've been arguing all the afternoon about whether or not we should consult you. It wasn't an easy decision to make — but — "

"Mr Barnard, whatever the problem is, it's better to have it out in the open," said Lucinda firmly. "We can't take any action if we don't know what's wrong."

"That's what we said," Lady Sarson assented, "but Dorothy Webb and Norman Poynter didn't agree. Norman thinks he might be mistaken, and Dorothy doesn't want to make a fuss."

"Please, Lady Sarson, Mr Barnard, what on earth has happened?" Lucinda appealed.

"I regret to say we believe there's a thief in our midst," said Barnard bluntly.

For a minute there was silence. Both the Cassidys were shocked. This was bad news. They could foresee a great deal of unpleasantness if the story were true.

Hugh Cassidy sighed. "You obviously have good reason for that remark, Mr Barnard. Perhaps you'd explain."

"Of course."

No one had paid much attention when Norman Poynter had lost his wallet. Norman was always mislaying his possessions. But the wallet had contained between forty and seventy-five pounds — Norman had not been sure of the exact amount — and it had not been found, though a very thorough search had been made and Norman was sure it must be somewhere in the house because he knew he had had it at lunch-time and he hadn't been out that afternoon.

Barnard had himself been the next apparent victim. Twenty pounds had disappeared from the wallet he had carelessly left on his bedside table when he went down for breakfast, or so he had at first been convinced. Then some doubt had crept into his mind. Was he absolutely certain of how much money the wallet had contained? And, as a result of his doubts, he hadn't mentioned the matter to anyone until yesterday.

Yesterday Dorothy Webb had lost thirty pounds, and today Melissa had lost a ring. 'Lost' in both cases was a euphemism. Neither woman had any doubt it was theft.

Dorothy had planned to go into Colombury that afternoon to buy a birthday present for her sister, and

Sarah had cashed a cheque for her for fifty pounds. Unfortunately she had left her handbag containing the money in the armchair where she had been sitting in the drawing-room before lunch. It was only minutes before she had missed it and returned to get it. For some unexplained reason she had counted the money at once.

"It wasn't the sort of thing she'd normally have done," said Melissa, "but it was lucky she did. And of course, she knew exactly how much should have been there."

"She's a very punctilious person," Hugh said. He saw no reason to tell Lady Sarson that a loss of that size would have been important to Miss Webb, who was not wealthy and certainly could not have afforded to come to Evenlode if her sister had not bought the apartment for her.

"Anyway, she was extremely upset about it," Melissa continued. "She doesn't drive, as you know, and I'd promised to give her a lift into Colombury. I thought she was going to cry in the car."

"Oh heavens, that's dreadful," Lucinda

said, instantly sympathetic.

"My dear Mrs Cassidy," Kenneth Barnard intervened. "If you don't mind my saying so, it's not Miss Webb's distress that's dreadful — after all thirty pounds are by the way. It's the evident fact that we have a thief — apparently an opportunist thief — at Evenlode."

"Quite." Hugh Cassidy controlled his irritation; he knew Barnard was right, but he resented his condescending attitude. "And you've lost a ring, Lady Sarson?" he said.

"It's been pinched, Dr Cassidy." Lady Sarson could, when she chose, be surprisingly downright. "Fortunately it's not particularly valuable. Costume jewellery, worth perhaps a hundred or a hundred and fifty, but I was fond of it. I put it in the box where I keep such things when I went to bed last night, and by mid-morning today it was gone."

"I see, Lady Sarson." Hugh wasn't prepared to ask her if she was sure of her facts. "Have you heard of anyone else who has lost money or property, that might in fact have been stolen?"

"No, but there's no reason why we

should. We haven't been asking other residents."

"So you've not discussed your losses with anyone, that is apart from Miss Webb and Mr Poynter?"

"We've mentioned the subject to Mrs Horne and Mrs Luton — and I'm afraid that's all we can tell you."

Hugh nodded. "Well, what can I say? Naturally my wife and I very much regret that this should have happened at Evenlode. Unless you wish us to notify the police immediately, we should like you to give us a day or two to consider the matter and make inquiries. Will you do that?"

"Of course. That's what we hoped you'd say," said Barnard. "We all agreed we didn't want the police. You know your staff — and your residents — better than anyone, and we thought perhaps you might be able to limit the number of possible suspects, and set some sort of trap for him — or her."

"We'll do our best — and we'll do it as quickly as we can," Hugh promised.

★ ★ ★

When the residents had gone the Cassidys stared at each other in mock despair. Lucinda shook her head and Hugh swore. This was not a situation they had ever imagined themselves facing.

"What are we going to do?" Lucinda asked.

"Think! Think damned hard," said Hugh. "It shouldn't be too difficult to trace the culprit. In fact, Barnard told us how to do it. It has to be someone who has access both to the reception rooms and the apartments themselves. If we eliminate the family, which of course we must — "

"And Val!"

"Val? Val Rowan? Come to think of it, Cindy, the troubles have started with her arrival."

"Hugh, that's rubbish. She could have had nothing to do with Norman Poynter's lost — stolen — wallet. She wasn't here when it happened."

"Nor she was. Good!" Hugh Cassidy gave his wife a rueful grin. "It boils down to the indoor staff, doesn't it? Cindy, I think we'd better have a family meeting to discuss the matter. It's only right they should be consulted and, who knows, one of them may have heard or seen something significant. Because, my dear, we've got to solve this unpleasant problem — and the sooner the better, or it could spoil the whole atmosphere of Evenlode."

3

"**I** REGRET to say it, but everything points to the Wilsons."

Hugh Cassidy looked from one young face to the next. Seemingly they had all been shocked by news of the thefts, except perhaps for Patrick to whom it had come more as an explanation than a surprise after the few words of conversation he had inadvertently overheard in the drawing-room. But he shared the general distress. There had been a series of petty thefts in one of the hotels in which he had trained; they had affected everyone, from the owners to the kitchen boy, and he appreciated how a similar series of occurrences at Evenlode would disturb the even tenor of the place.

"They must be sacked, and quickly," he said.

"Of course not!" Jill was horrified. "We've no actual proof they're guilty. The only evidence against them is circumstantial. It wouldn't be fair to dismiss them just like that."

"We've got to consider ourselves first."

"No! Why should we?" It was Jill who had been responsible for the presence of Mrs Wilson and her daughter, Zena, at Evenlode. By chance she had found them walking home from Colombury after missing the bus, and had given them a lift. At the time the Cassidys, who had recently moved into Evenlode, had been looking for domestic staff and the Wilsons had been thankful to exchange a long daily bus ride for a short bicycle trip. The arrangement had suited everyone and had worked well.

"We don't have any choice, Jill." Patrick was impatient with his wife. "We can't afford to be sentimental."

"There is such a thing as justice."

Hugh interrupted their bickering. "It's Evenlode we've got to consider," he said, "and, remember, that's not just ourselves. It's also — most importantly — all our residents."

No one argued with this. There was a moment's silence. Lucinda saw Simon exchange sympathetic smiles with Val;

Val had been chatting to him in his room when she had told him that there was to be a family meeting, and somehow it had been impossible to exclude her from the invitation. Hugh had raised no objection to her presence, and only Sarah had given her a long cool glance of disapproval.

"Then what do *you* propose we do, Dad?" Simon asked.

"Keep our eyes open, all of us. And, I have to say it, especially keep an eye on the Wilsons. They have served us well. They've often done extra and dirty jobs without complaint and they're not clock-watchers. We should be sorry to see them go."

"But — " Patrick prompted.

Hugh ignored him. "Jill's right. We can't sack them on mere suspicion. For one thing they could sue us for unfair dismissal. We must have concrete proof and therefore, although it's distasteful, I see no option but to set a trap for them — if it is them, or either of them. The obvious would be to leave a wallet or a handbag lying around and hope to catch a thief in the act. Failing that, we might mark a twenty-pound note and use that

41

as bait. I know it's unpleasant, but I don't think we have any choice."

And, as there were no other suggestions, this was agreed upon, with Jill the most reluctant and Patrick urging that there should be a minimum of delay.

★ ★ ★

For two days nothing happened. By agreement, Kenneth Barnard left his wallet on his bedside table each morning when he went down to breakfast, but the amount of money in it didn't vary. There was a little excitement on the second day when Norman Poynter announced that his watch had disappeared, but it was soon found in his dressing-gown pocket, where he had put it when he went for his daily pre-breakfast swim. The extraordinary relief this solution caused the Cassidys was a reflection of the stress they were under.

On the third day Lucinda put some marked banknotes in one of her handbags and instructed Jill to tuck it half under a cushion in the drawing-room when everyone had gone in to lunch. It was at this time of day that Mrs Wilson and her daughter were meant to plump up the cushions, collect any newspapers or magazines that might be lying around and generally tidy the room. The job only took a few minutes, and the idea was that Jill would do her best to keep an eye on the room for that short while. But Jill, who refused to believe the Wilsons were guilty and disliked the idea of trying to trap them, passed on the task to Val.

So it was Val who burst into the office where Sarah and Patrick were checking accounts. Patrick gave her an absent-minded smile, and Sarah a cold stare.

"What is it? We're busy."

"The Wilsons — or rather Zena. I'm not sure, but I think she's taken something from Mrs Cassidy's bag — the one that was put under the cushion in the drawing-room."

Patrick pushed back his chair. "Was Doreen — her mother — with her?"

"No, she was at the other end of the room."

"OK. I'll get Dad."

Patrick was back with Hugh within minutes. Sarah and Val hadn't spoken.

Patrick had collected Lucinda's bag, and while Val repeated what she had seen he counted the money. A marked twenty-pound note was missing.

"Thank goodness," he said. "Now we can finish this nasty business."

"Yes." Hugh was not looking forward to his interview with Mrs Wilson and her daughter. "Val, did you actually see Zena take anything from the bag?"

Val hesitated. "No, not actually. But she certainly picked it up and looked as if she was about to open it."

Hugh nodded. "All right, Patrick, you go and get them. Make them bring their bags. Sarah, you and Val had better leave us. We don't want this to appear to be a kind of court martial."

They went gladly and Hugh, left alone, sat down behind the desk, and automatically tidied the papers on it as he contemplated how to handle the matter. He didn't have long to wait. Patrick returned with the Wilsons, each carrying a hold-all. They looked puzzled rather than worried. Hugh waved them to chairs in front of him, and Patrick to a chair at the side of the room. He would have preferred to deal with the Wilsons by himself, but had decided that in the circumstances it would be advisable to have a witness.

"Mrs Wilson — Zena," he began, "during the last few days there have been some unpleasant happenings at Evenlode House. Several people have lost money and Lady Sarson has lost a ring that she treasured — "

"What's that to do with us? Dr Cassidy, you're not accusing us of stealing, are you?"

For a moment Hugh made no reply. It had occurred to him that Mrs Wilson had appreciated the situation extremely quickly. But, short and square, with brown boot-button eyes, Doreen Wilson was a shrewd, intelligent woman — unlike her daughter who, though similar in appearance, was mentally far inferior.

"I wonder, Mrs Wilson, if you'd be prepared to let my son-in-law examine the contents of your hold-alls?"

"I'm not sure we would, Dr Cassidy."

Mrs Wilson sounded aggressive, but Hugh's profession had taught him to be observant, and he noticed that her hands lying in her lap were tightly clenched. She was nervous.

"So far we've refrained from calling in the police, but I'm sure you realize that the matter has to be resolved. Especially as there was another theft from a handbag left in the drawing-room a short while ago."

"Well, I didn't see no handbag when I tidied the room." Mrs Wilson turned to her daughter who seemed to be studying her fingernails. "Did you, Zena?"

"Yes, I did, Mum. If it was a grey bag with a sort of fancy handle."

Doreen Wilson drew in a sharp breath. "You never mentioned it to me."

Zena shrugged. "Why should I? I didn't know about these thefts, did I? I thought the lady'd be coming back for her bag, and if I moved it she wouldn't know where it had gone. So I just left it where it was."

"You didn't take anything from the bag, Zena?" Hugh asked quietly.

"'Course not!"

She was so sure of herself that Hugh was almost convinced. Val had said she had seen Zena with Lucinda's bag in her hands; she hadn't actually seen Zena extract the note. But the note was missing.

"Then you won't mind if Mr Donne looks in your hold-all?"

Now Zena wasn't so sure. She glanced at her mother. "Mum?"

Doreen had made up her mind. "Why not? We've nothing to hide." She picked up her hold-all and emptied its contents on to the floor — a pair of outdoor shoes, a cardigan, a spectacle case, some rubber gloves, a thin wallet, a purse, a small cabbage, and surprisingly perhaps, a paperback novel.

"Mrs Cassidy gave me the cabbage," she said.

Hugh nodded. "And your bag, Zena," he said, as Patrick examined Mrs Wilson's wallet and purse.

Reluctantly, or so it seemed, Zena opened the hold-all that she had been clutching to her chest, and up-ended it as her mother had done. The contents were similar, except that instead of a paperback and a cabbage there was a bag of toffees which broke open and spilled all over the floor. The purse held some loose change, and there was no twenty-pound note in the wallet. At last Patrick shook his head at Hugh.

Doreen Wilson was triumphant. "Well, I hope you're satisfied, Dr Cassidy. I think you owe us both an apology. It's not nice for innocent people to be accused of thieving, you know."

"I realize that, Mrs Wilson, and — " Hugh began.

Patrick interrupted him. "Wait a minute! These hold-alls usually have side pockets that zip up."

He plucked Zena's hold-all from her lap. Sure enough, there was a pocket stretching the width of the back. He unzipped it and put in his hand. The first thing he produced was a crumpled banknote for twenty pounds. He placed it carefully on the desk, so that Hugh could see the condemning blob of red ink in the top right-hand corner. Here was all the evidence of Zena Wilson's guilt that was needed.

But more was to follow. Beside the bank note Patrick laid a leather wallet which bore in gold leaf the initials 'N.R.P.' Norman Poynter's money was no longer in it. Finally Patrick produced a small object wrapped in tissue paper. This was Lady Sarson's amethyst ring, and the sight of it loosened Zena's tongue.

"I never seen any of that stuff before — none of it! You can't pin it on me. I'm no thief." Zena stood up. She was shaking. "I never took those things, I tell you! I didn't! I didn't!"

"Zena!" It was like a slap in the face. Zena stared at her mother, open-mouthed. Then she sat down again and began to cry, great blubbering sobs which she made no effort to control. Doreen Wilson's normally ruddy face was scarlet. She was furiously angry. She turned on her daughter.

"You little bitch! I warned you that if this ever happened again I'd — "

They were not to know what Doreen Wilson would or would not do to her daughter. Hugh intervened. He shouted at them to shut up, and there was a moment's utter silence, broken only by a loud sniff from Zena.

"What did you mean by that, Mrs Wilson? Has Zena been in trouble before?"

Reluctantly Mrs Wilson said, "She took a couple of things from a store a few years ago, and she was warned then, though the owner didn't press charges. But the cop said if it happened again, she'd go to prison for sure, and she's not a bad girl really — "

Hugh considered. "I see," he said again. "Well, listen to me, both of you, while I tell you what I intend to do. Do you understand?" They nodded, for when he chose Hugh Cassidy could be an authoritative figure. "First, can either of you give me one good reason why I shouldn't hand Zena over to the police?"

"Not the police. Please, sir." Doreen Wilson's truculence had faded, as had her spurt of anger. "As I said, they'll send her to prison for sure, and it'll kill her. She's not a bad girl really," she repeated. "I thought I'd put the fear of God into her last time, but — "

"You'd better have another go, Mrs Wilson, or she *will* end up in prison. Because this isn't a question of yielding to a sudden temptation — it's systematic theft, and it can't be excused, least of all in a place like Evenlode House. However, I don't intend to call in the police. Mr Donne is going to see you off the premises, and we don't want you here again. I'll send you a cheque for what we owe you and, in view of the fact that you've worked well, the equivalent of a week's notice."

"Thank you, Dr Cassidy," said Mrs Wilson. "That's very generous of you. Zena, say thank you. You've been lucky, my girl."

Zena mumbled something which sounded to Patrick, who was helping to pick up the Wilsons' possessions from the floor, more like a repetition of her protestation of innocence than an expression of gratitude, but he made no comment. He saw off the Wilsons and returned to the office.

"They've gone, Dad."

"Good. I must say I didn't enjoy that interview, if that's what one should call it, especially when I started to have doubts about the girl's guilt."

"Well, we don't have to worry about that now."

"Thanks to you, Patrick. If you'd not

thought of the pocket in the hold-all she might have got away with it."

"Until she pinched something else. I wonder why she kept everything in that bag and brought it to and fro. So that her mother wouldn't find the stuff, I suppose."

"Presumably." Hugh rose rather wearily to his feet. "Patrick, we're going to break a Cassidy rule and have a drink in the middle of the day. We'll redistribute the property after lunch. And that'll be the end of a most unpleasant affair."

But they were not to relax for very long.

4

AT one in the morning approximately thirty-six hours later the telephone on Hugh Cassidy's bedside table trilled. Waking, he saw the red light on the instrument's base that indicated it was an internal call, and at this hour it had to be an emergency. He was already sliding out of bed as he lifted the receiver.

"Dr Cassidy here," he said softly, in the hope that he could deal with the situation alone and that there would be no need to rouse Lucinda.

"Doctor, this is Anne Horne. I'm sorry to phone you in the middle of the night, but I'm ill. I've been vomiting and I have diarrhœa."

"Mrs Horne, I'll be with you at once."

He switched on his bedside lamp, reached across the bed and shook Lucinda. "Wake up, love."

"What is it, Hugh?"

"Mrs Horne. Vomiting and diarrhœa.

53

It sounds like food poisoning."

"Oh God, I hope not! If it is there may be others ill too."

"You'd better come. Warn Simon and switch the phone through to him. Be as quick as you can. I'll go ahead." He pulled on slacks and a sweater over his pyjamas, and was checking his medical bag to make sure he had everything he might require. "Mrs Horne isn't one to make a fuss over nothing and she sounded dreadful."

"I'll be right with you."

Evenlode House had been built in the American style, long and low, with the residential apartments in what were known as the east and west wings. The centre block was given over to the entrance hall, reception rooms, offices and kitchen quarters on the ground floor, above which lived the family, including Sarah Field and now Val Rowan. There was a small, separate guest house.

Anne Horne's apartment was on the upper floor of the west wing, and Hugh Cassidy was able to ignore the lift, run along the corridor, unlock the connecting door between the Cassidys' private rooms and the residents' apartments and reach Mrs Horne only minutes after her phone call. He found her lying on top of her bed. She was pale and there were beads of perspiration on her forehead and upper lip, but she hadn't lost her sense of humour.

"I'm going to need to trot any moment, Dr Cassidy, so don't stand between me and the bathroom."

"I won't. How often have you had to do this?"

"Five or six times. I've lost count."

"That's too much. I'll give you an injection to stop it. And I'll leave you some powder to mix with water and drink when you've stopped vomiting."

"Good, but I must go again now."

Anne pushed herself off the bed and tottered hurriedly into the bathroom. As Hugh prepared the injection he could hear her retching into the lavatory pan and he frowned. This wasn't good for anyone, and for an elderly woman it was especially dangerous. Whatever the cause, the reaction put a strain on the heart. He wondered if anyone else was being sick.

Lucinda arrived as Anne returned to the bedroom. She helped her into bed, and Hugh gave her the injection.

"There you are, Mrs Horne, that should settle your inside. It should work quite quickly, but if it doesn't, don't hesitate to call me. And, if you feel you can manage it, I want you to drink this — it's only a solution of salt and sugar — but it'll help solve any dehydration problem. Think of it as a 'third world' remedy." He gave her the tumbler, and she drank it. He produced a couple of sachets and showed her how to mix a similar drink, when she felt up to it.

"You're very kind, both of you," she said.

"Not at all," said Lucinda. "That's what we're here for. Is there anything else you'd like? What about some tea?"

"That would be wonderful."

While Lucinda went into the kitchenette to make the tea, Hugh asked what Anne had eaten the previous day, hoping that she might have gone out for a meal which could be blamed for her sickness. She had not. The probability was, therefore, assuming this was some form of food poisoning, that dinner at Evenlode was responsible, or she would have been taken ill before. But it was impossible to pinpoint even a likely cause at this stage. They would have to await developments.

Lucinda came back with a tray of tea. "I'll look through the letter-boxes and see if there are lights showing in any of the other apartments, Hugh. I'll go outside and see if any windows are lit, too. If there are, others might be unwell."

"Fine," said Hugh. "I'll stay with Mrs Horne for a while."

"It's not necessary, my dear, I'm feeling so much better and you may be needed elsewhere."

"Are you sure, Mrs Horne?"

"Quite sure. Off you go, both of you."

"All right, but you must stay in bed in the morning. I'll be along to check on you. Doctor's orders," Hugh said.

★ ★ ★

After they left Anne Horne's apartment the Cassidys looked and listened for any sign that other residents were awake.

The only noise they heard came from Kenneth Barnard's suite at the end of the building. He came to the door as soon as they rang his bell.

"Good morning," he said. "This is an early call. What can I do for you? There's trouble?"

"I'm afraid so," Lucinda replied. "Mrs Horne has been taken ill. Her symptoms suggest possible food poisoning and, as you were awake, we wondered . . . "

She stopped. Barnard was nodding understanding and regretful agreement. He hadn't actually vomited or had diarrhœa, but he had felt distinctly queasy — as he put it — and had paid several uncomfortable though useless visits to the loo earlier in the night. By now, however, he was much improved and hoping to get some sleep. They were not to worry about him.

"That's nice to hear," said Lucinda, as he wished them a firm good night before closing the door on them.

"Let's be thankful he's no worse," said Hugh.

"Yes." Lucinda was tired. She worked hard seven days a week and the absence of the Wilsons had added to her burden. The idea of sleep was enticing. Usually optimistic, she couldn't help thinking that when she and Hugh were Barnard's age they would be lucky if they could afford half the comfort . . . Her thoughts were interrupted by the sight of Sarah who, in pyjamas and dressing-gown, was running down the corridor towards them.

"Simon sent me to find you." Sarah was slightly out of breath. "He's had a call from Miss Webb. She sounds desperately ill and half-hysterical. And as soon as he put the receiver down there was a call from Mrs Forster in the east wing. I went to wake Jill but she was already up. Patrick's sick too."

"Christ!" Hugh ran a hand through his hair. "This is a bad do. It'll have to be reported to the District Health Officer."

"It must be the food, something some, but not all of them, ate." Lucinda was trying to think logically.

"Don't worry about that now. We'll sort it out later. But we'd better take lab samples, and I'm not sure I should try to handle this alone. We'll have to see how many of them are hospital cases. Sarah, go back and help Simon. If there are any more phone calls say I'll be along as soon as I can. Get Jill to go to Mrs Forster. Patrick will have to cope by himself. You and I had better see after Miss Webb, Cindy."

★ ★ ★

There was no answer to Dorothy Webb's doorbell, and the Cassidys let themselves into her ground-floor apartment with a pass key. They found her lying on the carpet in the bathroom. Clearly she had felt the need to go to the lavatory, but she hadn't got there in time, and she lay in a pool of her own vomit, whimpering like a child. At least she was whimpering, thought Hugh. Quickly he checked her vital signs and decided against an immediate ambulance. The Cassidys exchanged glances, then set to work. It was not pleasant, taking samples for analysis, but they had dealt with worse in hospital.

Twenty minutes later Dorothy Webb, clean and sweet-smelling and in a fresh nightdress, was in bed. Hugh gave her a sedative and very soon she was almost asleep. Lucinda had done her best with the bathroom, but the carpet would require a thorough cleaning. There was nothing more they could do immediately except roll up Miss Webb's dirty nightdress and bed jacket and take them away to be laundered the next day.

Back in their apartment there was no chance to relax. Jill had made Mrs Forster comfortable and returned to Patrick, but meanwhile Simon had taken another call. Wearily the Cassidys went along to the west wing and, that call dealt with, looked in on Mrs Forster.

By the time they left her, as Lucinda said, it was scarcely worth while going to bed. But Hugh, knowing that they would have a hard day ahead of them, insisted that she and Sarah should try to get a couple of hours' sleep.

"What about you?" Lucinda asked.

"I'm too restless. I'll make myself a pot of tea and perhaps doze in a chair. I want to think about all this."

It was true, Hugh reflected, that he was too restless and too worried. There had been the unpleasant business of the thefts, and now what was probably an outbreak of food poisoning. Evenlode House seemed to have run out of luck.

* * *

There was every reason to worry as the day progressed. Altogether nine residents complained of having been more or less unwell in the course of the night. The obvious explanation was food poisoning. This the medically-minded Cassidys knew could bring misery and unmentionable distress at the time, but was rarely serious or life-threatening except to the very young or the very old; the trouble was that all the residents of Evenlode were elderly.

However, by the morning most of the sufferers were in fairly good health again. But they expected extra attention. One of the reasons they had come to Evenlode and were prepared to pay highly for the services it offered was that they could receive every care if they were not feeling at their best. And, after all, though no one mentioned the fact, on this occasion it looked as if the Cassidys were to blame for their indispositions.

As a result, the Cassidys were kept busy tending the sick and the not so sick — and this in addition to their normal chores. Luckily Patrick was the only member of the family who had suffered from the poisoning but, apart from Val, they had all been up most of the night and as the day wore on they became progressively more exhausted, and tempers frayed.

If Sarah had gone into the office on a normal afternoon and found Val using the phone, she might have shown some resentment but she would not have burst out with, "What the hell do you think you're doing?"

"Telephoning," Val said coldly, taken aback by the sudden attack.

"You've no right to use this phone without asking. Was it long distance? You're not supposed to know anyone locally. That's why Simon brought you here, because you had nowhere nearby to go."

"And how clear you make it that you wish he hadn't."

"What do you mean by that?"

63

"Isn't it obvious, Sarah? You resent me, don't you? You're jealous."

Passing the door, Simon heard raised voices and came into the office. "What on earth's going on here? You can be heard at the other end of the building."

The two girls turned and glared at him, as if their quarrel was his fault — which in a sense it was. Sarah, very pale, her eyes bright, was trembling with anger. Val was much more controlled, but her cheeks were flushed.

"Oh, Simon, it's so silly," she said, "but Sarah's furious with me because I was using the telephone in here. I didn't know I shouldn't use this phone."

"Of course you can use the phone," Simon said. He grinned at her. "But you'll have to pay if you run up huge bills speaking to China or South America."

Val laughed. "I won't do that," she promised, her composure completely restored. She ignored Sarah and addressed herself to Simon. "I was just phoning my girl-friend in Oxford, the one I expected to share a flat with. She asked me to have lunch with her next Saturday. Will that be all right?"

"I'm sure it will. Perhaps I could give you a lift."

"Thanks, Simon, but I can catch the bus."

While this conversation was taking place Sarah had turned her back on the others and was pretending to be busy at the desk. When she heard the office door open and shut she thought they had both gone, and was surprised when Simon spoke.

"Sarah, I want to say something to you — about Val. Just stop being bitchy to her! Do you understand? No one could have worked harder or been more helpful today than she has and — "

"Go to hell!" Sarah said.

But when the door had opened and shut again and Simon had gone, she put her head down on the desk and wept.

★ ★ ★

The next overt display of temper among the Cassidys occurred after dinner. Lucinda, appalled at the idea of so many sick elderly residents and aware of her personal responsibility, had among

65

her other duties of the day been determined to trace the probable cause of the food poisoning. This had not proved difficult, though actual proof was impossible. There was no left-over food — the remains had gone into the garbage disposal unit, and all the plates, glasses and cutlery had been through the dishwasher. But the previous evening for dinner she had made three large veal and mushroom casseroles for the main course. Once the rest of the meal was exonerated, the probability was high that one of these casseroles — and only one of them — was to blame. This would account for the fact that not everyone had been taken ill. The difficulty with this theory, however, was Patrick, who had shared the family casserole, for there was no question but that he had been very sick. Indeed, he was still unwell and had eaten hardly anything all day.

Jill chided him. "It's not like you, Patrick. You usually can't get enough food to satisfy that skinny frame of yours."

It was then that Lucinda expounded her theory, and its problem. Patrick stared at her in amazement.

"That's it!" he said. "There's no difficulty. There was some gravy and mushrooms left over from one of the other casseroles and when I was helping to clear up after dinner I — I finished it off!"

"You greedy shit!" said Jill and, ignoring her mother's remonstrance, continued, "When I think how sorry for you I was last night — and it was all your own fault."

"It was not my fault. I didn't expect to be poisoned. And anyway, you weren't very sympathetic — not half as sympathetic as Sarah. There I was, being as sick as a dog, and you — "

Hugh banged the arm of his chair. "Shut up!" he shouted. "Stop bickering, both of you!"

There was immediate silence. Hugh Cassidy was on the whole an even-tempered man, and this outburst of his had shocked them. But he had had less sleep than anyone the previous night and his patience had been sorely taxed during the day.

"Now," he continued quietly, "we

haven't had much sleep in the last twenty-four hours and it hasn't been the easiest of days. We're all fraught. So let's forget about the casseroles for the present. We should know more once those samples that I took have been analysed. In the meantime, let's go to bed, though it's early. That's what I propose to do. With luck — and we deserve some luck for a change — we'll get a reasonable amount of rest tonight and tomorrow will be a brighter and happier day for everyone at Evenlode."

For a moment there was no response. Then Simon said, "Coming from you, Dad, that was quite a speech."

The remark broke the tension. Hugh laughed and said that it had been directed at himself as well as everyone else. But he was standing up, and so was Lucinda. No one doubted that Dr Cassidy meant what he had said.

5

BY the next day, after a good night's sleep, everyone was more cheerful. Those who had not been ill no longer expected to be stricken, and those who had suffered were all well on their way to total recovery — even Miss Webb. The general inclination now was to make light of the incident. No one wanted to blame the Cassidys, and they were loudly praised for the care and consideration they had shown.

Nevertheless, the residents were eager to gossip about the matter and, when the mushrooms were named as the possible culprit, a spate of stories emerged, some of them horrendous, for who hasn't known or read about someone who has died a ghastly death from eating the wrong kind of fungi? And, inevitably, the news of the food poisoning spread beyond Evenlode House, so that no one thought to inquire from where Michael Balham had obtained his information.

But, at about eleven o'clock, sooner than might have been expected, Michael Balham strode purposefully into the entrance hall of Evenlode House. He had fair hair, blue eyes that matched his blouson jacket and a boyish grin, but his good looks were spoilt by a self-satisfied expression. Sarah, who was sitting at the reception desk checking an account for Patrick, was not impressed.

"May I help you?" she asked.

"I sincerely hope so. My name's Michael Balham and I'm on the *Colombury Courier*. You may have seen my by-line. I'm sure you must read our paper."

At the mention of the local newspaper, Sarah instantly became wary. "Not often," she said.

"Really?" His eyes widened. "What you're missing! You should remedy that, Miss — ?"

Sarah did not volunteer her name. "What can I do for you, Mr Balham?"

His grin widened. "I can imagine a lot of pleasurable things, sweetie, but not right now. It's quite the wrong time and the wrong place."

"Don't be offensive! Just what do you

want?" Sarah demanded.

"A story. A little bird told me you've been having your troubles here. Half your geriatrics down with food poisoning and — "

"Mr Balham, there are no *geriatrics* at Evenlode House. Your little bird has misinformed you."

"And no food poisoning? Salmonella or something like that? Nothing worse, I hope. How many are ill?"

"Mr Balham, will you please go away? There's no story for you here. As I said, you've been misinformed."

"No, I don't think so, sweetie. You're trying to cover up." He paused. "Ah, here's someone who might be more forthcoming."

Kenneth Barnard was approaching the reception desk, smiling at Sarah; he wanted a bulky letter to be weighed. Balham went towards him, hand outstretched.

"Good morning, sir. How are you?"

Barnard accepted the proffered hand, but was aware of Sarah shaking her head violently behind Balham's back, and clearly trying to convey some message to

71

him. "Good morning," he said. "I am well — and you?"

Slightly taken aback, Balham said, "I'm fine, thanks. But you, you've recovered?"

"I haven't been ill. What makes you think I have?"

"We heard about the food poisoning here."

"Really?" Balham looked inquiringly at Sarah.

"He's a reporter from the *Colombury Courier*," she said. "I've told him to go away, but he won't."

"I only want the answers to a few questions," Balham said. "How many people were taken ill? Have they all recovered? Was anyone bad? Did Dr Cassidy call in another doctor, or did he rely on his own judgement? Have you traced what caused the epidemic?"

"There was no epidemic, and there's no story," Sarah said angrily. "Get out!"

"No need to be shirty. I'm only doing my job."

"You've done it," Barnard said firmly. "Now, do as the lady says, and get out! Or do you want me to complain to the editor of your rag and demand he sacks you?"

"He wouldn't." Balham grinned. "My uncle's John Rayner and he's a director of the *Courier*. But not to worry. I'm going." And with a wave of his hand he strode out of the hall.

Kenneth Barnard stared after him in disgust. "What a singularly unpleasant young man," he said.

Unfortunately Melissa Sarson and another resident, meeting Michael Balham as he was making for his car, did not agree with Barnard's opinion of him, and they answered all his questions.

★ ★ ★

When Hugh Cassidy passed through the hall a little later, Sarah called to him and told him about the reporter from the *Courier*, and his conversations with the residents. "I'm sorry," she said, "if I'd thought I should have guessed he might meet some of the oldies as he was leaving. I should have seen him off the premises."

"My dear, it wasn't your fault. Barnard's

a sensible man. He'd know we wouldn't want any publicity about the food poisoning, but you can't stop people talking — especially elderly ladies."

Sarah laughed. "Do you know John Rayner, Balham's uncle?"

"Yes, slightly. He lives not far from here, near Chadlington. He's a property developer, but he has fingers in lots of pies. He's quite influential."

"I see," said Sarah thoughtfully. "That's a pity."

"It is, rather. Incidentally, I've just phoned the place where we got those mushrooms. It was difficult to be tactful about it, but the chap was very understanding. After all, we're good customers. But he said he couldn't explain it. There haven't been any other complaints, and the whole batch of mushrooms he sold that day came from the same commercial grower. So that's that! There's nothing more we can do until we get the lab reports on the samples, and that may take days. They're very busy, and if it's something not very obvious . . . Still, everyone's fine again now, even poor Miss Webb. So let's hope there won't be any repercussions, and we'll soon be able to forget the whole affair."

Unfortunately Hugh's hope was not to be fulfilled. He had scarcely finished speaking when Sarah's telephone burred. The voice at the other end of the line was so strident and demanding that Sarah had no need to relay the peremptory message; Hugh had heard it. Mrs James Grey wished to speak to Dr Cassidy at once, concerning her sister, Miss Dorothy Webb.

"Certainly, Mrs Grey," Sarah said sweetly. "I'll see if he's available." She covered the mouthpiece and looked at Hugh. "Are you available, Dr Cassidy?"

Hugh nodded and took the receiver. "Good morning, Mrs Grey. Dr Cassidy here."

And now it was Sarah's turn to listen as Hugh, wincing, held the receiver away from his ear while Mrs Grey delivered her tirade. Briefly, though Mrs Grey was the reverse of brief, she had been informed that there had been an outbreak of food poisoning at Evenlode House. She had immediately telephoned her sister, who had confirmed that she had been ill and, Mrs Grey was at some pains to point out, she did not pay vast sums of money on behalf of her sister for third-rate care and attention!

Hugh Cassidy listened and apologized. There was nothing else he could do; he could scarcely tell Mrs Grey to go to hell when, as she said, she paid the bills for her sister. They should never have accepted Dorothy Webb, he thought, not on these terms, but Miss Webb had been so pathetic and eager to come. He was sure that she herself hadn't complained.

"Mrs Grey," he said when the lady seemed to have finished what she had to say, "how did you learn about our trouble here?"

"Ashley Ormonde told me." Perhaps surprised by the question, Mrs Grey answered without hesitation. "He happened to be in the office of the *Courier* when someone phoned in the news."

"Mr Ormonde's a friend of yours?"

"Actually I hardly know him, but his wife and I sit on the same Oxfam committee. Why do you ask?"

"I just wondered," said Hugh Cassidy.

What he was really wondering was why Ashley Ormonde seemed to go out of his way to cause the Cassidys trouble when they had never done him any harm.

* * *

Feeling depressed by his conversation with Mrs Grey and the thought of the bad publicity Evenlode would receive if there was a snide article in the *Courier*, Hugh had to make an effort to respond to Morag Luton, who waved to him to join her when, a while later, he entered the drawing-room. But she was obviously so elated that his own spirits rose.

"Wonderful news, Dr Cassidy! Wonderful news!" She was pink with pleasure. "You'll never guess."

"Do I have to try, Mrs Luton?" Hugh smiled at her.

"It's my nephew, Angus — the professor at Carleton University in Ottawa. I've just been telling Mrs Horne and Mr Poynter here." She gestured at her companions. "He's in England, Dr Cassidy, in Oxford.

He's coming to see me."

"Why, that's great," said Hugh, "and what a surprise."

"Yes, it is a surprise. I was astonished when he phoned. He said he'd written to me, but I haven't had the letter yet."

"The post from North America is dreadful, very erratic," remarked Norman Poynter. "Letters from my son in Washington take anything from one to three weeks to reach me."

"Well, it doesn't matter. He's here now!" Morag made no attempt to contain her delight. "Or he will be tomorrow, right here at Evenlode House. I wonder if I'll recognize him. I haven't seen him for years."

"But you've that fine studio photograph of him in your sitting-room," said Anne Horne.

"That was taken at least five years ago. He may have changed, though not much, I don't expect."

"Do you want to reserve one of the guest rooms for him?" Hugh asked.

"No, not for the moment. He's staying with a fellow don from Christ Church. I gather he's in Oxford in connection with his academic work. He said he'd explain when he saw me. But he expects to be in England for several weeks, so perhaps when his business is over . . . " Morag smiled hopefully up at Hugh.

"Of course, Mrs Luton. We should be delighted."

"And about tomorrow. He has to have lunch with some professor or other, but he'll be here for tea and dinner, and I thought it would be nice if I gave a small drinks party for him, just half a dozen people at about six o'clock. Perhaps Mrs Cassidy would make us a few of those delicious little nibbles of hers, and if one of the young could help . . . "

"Of course, Mrs Luton," Hugh said again. "A pleasure."

And he thought what a liar he was. It had been a hell of a week with one crisis after another. They were still short staffed, and the last thing they needed was extra work on a Saturday, when residents often asked guests to dinner. 'Delicious little nibbles' didn't materialize at the wave of a wand, and if 'one of the young' was required in Mrs Luton's apartment it would mean extra pressure all round.

For the first time since they had taken the plunge and committed themselves to Evenlode, Dr Hugh Cassidy seriously doubted the wisdom of their decision. The euphoria which had seen them through the place's teething troubles had passed, but everything had seemed to be going smoothly until . . .

He wandered around the drawing-room, making bright conversation with those of the residents already gathered for their pre-luncheon drinks. Then, duty done, he went to break the news of Morag Luton's party to Lucinda.

★ ★ ★

When Hugh had left them Norman Poynter grinned and said, "Are Anne and I invited to your party, Morag?"

"Naturally!" Morag shot him a glance from her bright brown eyes. "I was well brought up, Norman Poynter, even if you weren't, and I wouldn't have dreamed of mentioning a party in front

80

of you if I'd not intended to invite you."

The little man chuckled. "Your poor nephew. What a party he's going to get! I hope he likes 'oldies', as the Cassidys call us behind our backs."

"Don't be provocative, Norman," said Anne. "I'm sure it'll be a good party and, after all, Angus is coming to see Morag, not us, but I'm sure he'll like to meet her friends."

"Of course he will," Norman said earnestly, but there was a quaver of amusement in his voice. "So who else are you thinking of asking, Morag?"

"Melissa Sarson and Kenneth Barnard and — " She named another couple. "I want to keep it small."

"I suppose you wouldn't consider including Dorothy Webb?" Anne was tentative. "She was sicker than anyone with this food poisoning, and I'm sure she'd appreciate the opportunity to socialize again."

"Besides, think how she'll make the party go." Norman couldn't resist the jibe. "She'll be the life and soul — "

"Norman!"

"Sorry, m'dear."

Morag Luton was a kind woman, and she leapt at Anne Horne's suggestion with alacrity. "What a good idea!" she said. "Of course I'll ask Dorothy."

6

"ANYONE like to volunteer?" Hugh Cassidy asked.

"What about you, Val?" said Sarah. "You and Mrs Luton seem to get on well together."

"Val's going to Oxford today to have lunch with her girlfriend there," Simon said.

"So she is. I'd forgotten," Sarah lied happily.

"But I'll be back before five." Val was quick. "I won't offer to help make the small eats, but I can certainly pass them around and serve drinks for Mrs Luton's guests."

"It would be a big help, dear," Lucinda said. "We've a full house for dinner tonight, and four extras — five including Mrs Luton's nephew. So, thanks."

She looked down the kitchen table. "Everyone finished breakfast?"

There were nods of assent and Jill said, "Even Patrick. He's obviously well again, since his appetite's returned."

"And a good thing too," said Patrick among the general laughter.

* * *

The reference to the food poisoning had reminded Hugh that after the visit of Mr Balham the previous day, there would probably be some mention of the incident in the local paper. He seized on it as soon as the daily newspapers arrived. His heart sank at once. There on the front page of the *Courier* was a large photograph of Evenlode House. The caption beneath read: 'Outbreak of food poisoning at luxury residence. See page 3.'

Hurriedly Hugh turned to page 3, and his worst fears were realized. The article, under the by-line of Michael Balham, spread across the whole page. It was headed: 'Should places like Evenlode House be allowed to exist?'

Gritting his teeth, Hugh read on. The piece began with a description of Evenlode, its grounds and its amenities, such as the heated swimming pool with its retractable roof. It was not unfair, though emphasis was laid on the luxurious living conditions that its residents enjoyed. Much was made of the delicious out-of-season food and the expensive wines that were served, and there was a statement (not true) that more was spent on flowers in a week than many a poor man with a family might earn in the same period.

And was it right, the article went on to ask, that twenty or so very rich old people should enjoy all these privileges? Would not Evenlode have better served the community if it had become a home for the not-so-rich, or the disabled, or for orphans? Could not badly needed housing have been built in the extensive grounds? Was not its present use extravagant and wasteful?

Granted that Evenlode provided a living — a good living — for Dr Cassidy and his family and a certain number of staff, Balham continued, would they not have been better employed elsewhere? It was surely a pity that Hugh Cassidy, a highly qualified doctor, should have abandoned the National Health Service for doubtless more remunerative but definitely less worthwhile work.

What was more, though hearts might not bleed for these excessively rich 'oldies', at least they should get a square deal. And were they getting it? The answer to that was a resounding 'No!'

For example, in the last few weeks they had had property stolen, and had been given unhygienic food. The thefts had been traced, but not the origin of the epidemic of food poisoning which had made so many of them ill. Considering the vast sums that they had originally paid for the privilege of moving into Evenlode House, and the exorbitant charges levied on them for what should be all the comforts of home, it was clear these 'oldies' had indeed got a poor deal.

Slowly Hugh closed the newspaper. It was a vicious piece, far worse than anything he had expected. The fact that there was an inherent contradiction in it didn't matter. By the time the reader had reached the end he would have half forgotten that he had started by disliking Evenlode House for providing extreme luxury for a few filthy rich people when the place could have been better used for those more deserving, and would be feeling indignant at the way the money-grabbing Cassidys treated these very same souls.

Tucking the *Courier* under his arm, he went to find Lucinda. He was waylaid by Melissa Sarson, who was brandishing another copy of the local paper.

"Dr Cassidy, have you read the disgusting article in this rag?" Lady Sarson didn't wait for an answer. "I do hope you don't blame me. I did tell that wretched little reporter about the food poisoning. Actually he seemed to know all about it already, and I insisted that we were all better. But I never mentioned the thefts, and as for suggesting that you treat us badly — dear Lord! The absolute reverse! You couldn't be kinder to us. It's — it's wonderful here."

Large blue eyes stared at Hugh out of Lady Sarson's ravaged old face, and her voice shook with emotion. For a moment Hugh thought she was going to cry, and he wondered irrelevantly if her mascara would run. But he was touched by her reaction.

"Thank you," he said. "Thank you. That's very comforting. I hope everyone feels the same."

"I'm sure they do. Don't worry, Dr Cassidy. You're just going through a bad patch. It will pass."

Smilingly, she left him, and Hugh told himself that she was probably right, but there was something about the article, apart from the unfair accusations, that worried him. And it was not merely the vindictiveness of the reporter.

Lucinda put her finger on it. "This chap Balham seems to know a great deal about Evenlode. Where do you think he got his information?"

"I don't know," Hugh said slowly, thinking that his wife indeed had a point; the article was extraordinarily detailed. Of course, the residents talked among themselves and with their local friends and acquaintances. Some of them knew they were referred to by the affectionate term of 'oldies'. And gossip soon spread. Nevertheless . . .

"Maybe Lady Sarson said more to that damned Balham man than she remembers," Lucinda suggested as an answer to her own question.

"I doubt it." Hugh was abrupt. "Melissa Sarson is old, but there's nothing wrong with her mind. She was and she still is an intelligent woman."

Lucinda sighed. Cold-fingered, she continued to fashion the pastry she was making. Her thoughts were on lunch, dinner, Mrs Luton's little party for her nephew. It was an awfully unfortunate article, but was it important? Obviously the reporter man had had a tip-off, and when he came to Evenlode to check it out perhaps Sarah hadn't been as tactful as she might have been, so that he had taken his frustration out on the establishment.

"It's a bloody article, I agree," she said, "but all we can do is ignore it, Hugh."

"I suppose you're right, but — "

"Darling, try to forget it, or at least don't let it worry you. We've a hard day ahead and other things to cope with. For one, you'd better be on hand to greet this Professor Luton when he arrives this afternoon. Remember this is a great occasion for one 'oldie'. She hasn't seen him for ages, and he's her only living relative."

"Let's hope he won't be a disappointment to her."

"Why on earth did you say that, Hugh?"

"I don't really know." Hugh shook his head. "But it's a bit pathetic how chuffed she is about his visit. Trite but true, money doesn't necessarily bring happiness."

"Nevertheless it's a very useful commodity. So you go and earn some, Hugh Cassidy, and let me get on with my work."

"OK."

Obediently Hugh did as he was asked and left Lucinda to her cooking, but he didn't find it as easy to accept her other admonition. He could not forget Balham's article in the *Colombury Courier*, and throughout the morning he continued to brood about it.

★ ★ ★

The young man came through the front door of Evenlode House, glanced about him with interest and advanced to the reception desk. He smiled, showing white and uneven teeth. "Professor Luton, to visit Mrs Luton," he announced formally, but unnecessarily.

Hugh had recognized him at once from the photograph in Morag's apartment, though it flattered the man, as such studio portraits are meant to do. There was the same dark hair, narrow face and moustache, but Angus Luton looked younger than Hugh had expected, and not nearly as glamorous. The head and shoulders likeness had disguised his stocky build, and the brown suit Luton was wearing did nothing for him. But he was out-going and pleasant.

"Welcome to Evenlode, Professor Luton," Hugh said. "Your aunt's expecting you. I'm Dr Cassidy, incidentally."

"I could have guessed." Luton held out his hand. "Auntie's often mentioned you and your wife in her letters — and with gratitude. She's very happy here."

"I'm glad. I'll show you up to her apartment."

"Number three, west wing!" Luton laughed. "You see, I know. You'd be surprised how much I do know about this place, Doctor. So if you'll just point me to the elevator, I won't need to bother you."

"It's no bother. I'll take you." Hugh came out from behind the reception desk. "Are you likely to be staying in England long, Professor?"

"I'm not sure. It all depends on what I can organize in Oxford. I'd certainly like to spend a year at the university here."

"I hope you will, then. It would delight your aunt." Hugh gestured the younger man into the waiting lift.

Luton hesitated. "Oh, I've left my automobile outside. I wasn't sure where to park it. Perhaps someone would show me or do it for me. The keys are in the ignition."

"Of course. I'll run it around to the garages myself."

"Many thanks."

After depositing Professor Luton at the front door of Morag's apartment, Hugh decided to move the car before he went to inspect a drystone wall that bordered the estate and had been damaged, supposedly by a lorry that had failed to stop. He went outside and, as he got into Luton's hired Ford Escort, he saw with relief that Val

92

was walking up the drive; Lucinda had been afraid that she might not get back from Oxford in time to help with Mrs Luton's party. Hugh waved to her and, smiling, she returned his wave. She was a nice girl, he thought, and attractive; it wasn't surprising that Simon was so taken with her, even though it was hard on Sarah.

Hugh parked the car and was about to get out of it when he noticed a small square of cambric with flowers embroidered in one corner on the floor — undoubtedly a lady's handkerchief. Thinking that Professor Luton hadn't wasted much time since coming to England, he left it on the seat.

★ ★ ★

Anne Horne was the first guest to arrive at Morag's party, but the others were close on her heels, and Val was kept busy, pouring drinks and passing around Lucinda's small eats. There was a buzz of happy conversation. Inevitably Angus Luton was the centre of attention with his aunt beside him, unable to hide her pride and joy at his presence. But he carried off the situation well, teasing her a little when she boasted about his achievements and mocking himself without false modesty.

"I guess that a professor at my university, Carleton, isn't comparable with a professor at Christ Church College, say. The former's far more lowly. In North America we all call ourselves professor once we have tenure."

"What's tenure?" asked Norman Poynter.

"Permanency. You can't be fired unless you commit some heinous crime." There was general laughter and Luton said, "But tell me more about Evenlode. You've a great set-up here, it seems to me."

"You wouldn't think so if you'd read today's local paper," said Melissa Sarson tartly.

The conversation then turned to Balham's feature, and required a long explanation to which Luton listened with sympathy. It was interrupted by a ring at the apartment door. The late arrival was Dorothy Webb, very apologetic; she had decided to have a little rest and had fallen asleep.

Morag, who had forgotten Dorothy was coming, immediately made a fuss of her. She introduced her nephew, showed Dorothy the bird carved from stone that he had brought her as a present from Canada, and dispatched Val to bring sherry and canapés. Dorothy, unused to such consideration, was even more gauche and direct than usual.

"You look very young for a professor, Mr Luton," she said, almost accusingly.

"That," said Angus Luton, straight-faced, "is because I've cut off my beard, Miss Webb."

Dorothy appeared not to see the joke. "What is your subject?" she asked.

"My subject?"

"Yes. What do you teach? I assume you do some teaching in addition to your research, Professor."

"Oh yes. I teach Canadian history — an honours course."

Anne joined them. She felt responsible for Dorothy's presence, as it was at her suggestion that she had been invited, and it was obvious to her that Angus Luton

95

was not greatly enjoying Miss Webb's company. She was in time to hear Dorothy say, "It surprises me that you speak of Eskimos. It's not a term I would have expected a Canadian academic to have used."

"What would you have expected?" Anne asked.

"I gather the proper name for those people is Inuit," said Dorothy.

"Really?" said Anne, who had known this perfectly well. "What a funny word." She turned to Angus Luton. "When may we hope to see you at Evenlode again?"

"Maybe for dinner one night, Mrs Horne, and with any luck next weekend too. Auntie's asked me to stay. She showed me the guest rooms when she was taking me round the place after tea and, if it's OK by Dr Cassidy, I'd sure love to spend two or three days here."

"We'll look forward to seeing more of you, then."

"Yes, indeed."

Anne smiled wryly. She couldn't blame Angus Luton for the lack of enthusiasm she detected in his voice. Apart from Val, there was no one in the room who could not have been his parent, if not his grandparent. It was good of him, she thought, to spare Morag a whole weekend from what was almost certainly a busy schedule, though of course that was the charitable view; he could have been thinking of what he might inherit from a rich aunt. Certainly Morag appreciated his attention.

* * *

Indeed Morag was still glowing with pleasure the next day. Everyone felt bound to compliment her on Professor Luton, and say what a pleasant young man he was. If one or two, such as Lady Sarson and Kenneth Barnard, had not been too impressed by him, they kept their thoughts to themselves. And the Cassidys were only thankful that for Morag's sake, everything had turned out well, and she hadn't been disappointed in her nephew.

7

THE following week began auspiciously. There were several letters to the *Courier* commenting on Michael Balham's feature on Evenlode House, but most of them were critical of what he had written, and the story was fast losing currency. Lucinda Cassidy had found a new cleaning woman to replace the sacked Zena Wilson so that, with Val's help, the work-load was once again reasonably normal. What was more, there had been no recurrence of any food poisoning. Nor had Ashley Ormonde complained again about the tree he was convinced was about to fall across his property, and fortunately the Cassidys' insurance policy would cover repairs to the drystone wall supposedly damaged by the lorry that hadn't stopped, and whose driver the Colombury police hadn't been able to trace.

This run of good fortune lasted till Wednesday.

★ ★ ★

Every morning Norman Poynter went for a swim before breakfast. This Wednesday was no exception. Mr Poynter was seventy-four. Short, with a red face, innocent blue eyes and white hair worn like a monk's tonsure, his appearance was misleading. He had been an astute and highly successful businessman. Now, a widower for the second time with his family grown up and scattered, Evenlode House suited him perfectly.

Though he could have used the pool during the day, and often did, he preferred it in the early morning when he could have the place to himself. It was his custom to put on his swimming trunks and towelling robe in his apartment and go downstairs between half past six and seven. Often he met no one or, if he did, it would only be a member of the family.

A solid door, locked and bolted, led from the house to the pool area. This was glazed on three sides and, when the sliding doors were adjusted and the roof retracted, it needed no imagination to believe oneself outside in the garden. Potted plants and garden furniture helped the illusion and — a big advantage — cold breezes could never spoil a summer's day. The Cassidys didn't regret either the architect's fees or the expense of building the pool. The oldies, in spite of their no longer youthful figures, loved this addition to Evenlode and made full use of it.

But for Norman Poynter nothing was more enjoyable than his early and solitary swim. As he turned the key in the lock and drew back the bolts this Wednesday morning he was looking forward to his first plunge into the cold — but not too cold — water. He wondered if for once he would dare to go in head first. He had never learnt to dive and, by modern standards, was only a moderate swimmer. Nevertheless he loved to traverse the pool with his slow steady breast stroke, head and shoulders held well above water, or, when the roof was retracted, to float on his back, staring up at the sky.

Today, as he stepped in anticipation into the pool area, he was struck by an overpowering smell that he identified at once. Chlorine — essential for keeping the water sweet and germ-free, but intended to be used in moderation. Apparently something had gone wrong with the automatic supply. It was a moment before he realized that this was not the only thing wrong.

Acting instinctively, Norman had pushed the door shut behind him and, handkerchief hurriedly pressed to his nose and mouth, he started to advance to the edge of the pool. Now he took in the fact that all around him was chaos. Tables and chairs had been overturned. Plants had been pulled out of their pots, some of which were broken, and scattered in the water. One of the glass doors had been smashed. To Norman it looked liked mindless vandalism, but he had little time to contemplate the scene.

He thought he heard a sound behind him and half turned. The next moment he had overbalanced and was floundering in the evil-smelling water. Hampered by his robe, he went under and came up, choking, his eyes smarting, but somehow he managed to struggle to the steps and haul himself from the pool. As he did, collapsing on the edge, he knocked off his spectacles which had somehow remained attached to him throughout and heard them skittle across the tiles.

Norman Poynter swore loudly, but there was no one to hear him. Without his spectacles, although he could see a certain amount, he felt at a loss, especially as his eyes were smarting from the chlorine and he was suffering some respiratory distress as the gas reached his lungs. Making a brief effort to wring out the lower half of his gown he stumbled to the door and, slamming it behind him, set off uncertainly along the corridor. He was more shocked than he would have admitted.

"Mr Poynter! What's the matter? What's happened?" Simon had seen him fumbling his way like a blind man, and came running. "Have you had an accident?"

"I've lost my spectacles."

Simon bit his lip to prevent a grin. Mr Poynter was always losing things, more often than not his spectacles, which is why he usually carried a second pair with him. "But you had them by the pool?"

"Yes. I knocked them off climbing out. Simon!" Norman seized him by the arm. "The pool's been vandalized. The whole place is a shambles and stinks of chlorine."

"Oh God!" Simon said, as he took in the situation.

Now he could smell the chlorine on Norman Poynter's robe and in his hair, and he realized that the little man was soaking wet. He'll get pneumonia, he thought, and in any case chlorine was a poisonous gas. With relief Simon saw his father in the distance and shouted to him. Hurriedly he gave a brief explanation.

"Right," Hugh said, hiding his dismay at yet another disaster. "I'll look after Mr Poynter. Simon, check the chlorine pump and turn it right off. Then open the roof and all the doors to the garden. And put a large notice on the door from the house saying the pool's out of order. We'll clear everything up later."

"No!" said Norman Poynter sharply, and when the two Cassidys stared at him, "No!" he said again. "This was a deliberate act of vandalism. You must call the police before you touch anything.

If nothing else, it will cover you with the insurance." He broke off as he started to choke.

"Mr Poynter, the first thing is to get you back to your room, and I'll examine you to make sure you've had no ill effects," Hugh protested. "And in any case we've had enough bad publicity recently."

"I know, but no one can blame you for this. Much better not to try to hush it up."

"I expect you're right. But come along, Mr Poynter. You need some practical care. We must wash out your eyes and look at your mouth if you swallowed any of the over-chlorinated water — and listen to your chest. Anyway, you won't be popular if you go on smelling of chlorine. Simon will bring up your spectacles. Let's hope they're not broken."

★ ★ ★

Norman Poynter seemed to have escaped fairly lightly. Dr Cassidy dealt with his eyes, produced a mild antiseptic mouthwash for some slight ulceration but luckily could find no trace of irritation in his lungs; nor did Poynter complain of any gastric distress. Hugh prescribed a hot bath and then bed, at least for the rest of the morning. His breakfast would be brought up to him.

Then, having consulted his wife, he took Poynter's advice and telephoned the Colombury police station, with the result that Sergeant Donaldson and PC Gorman arrived at Evenlode House in mid-morning. Donaldson was a stiffbacked officer, fairly recently promoted, and conscious of his own importance. He listened to Dr Cassidy's story, inspected the damaged pool and the chlorine pump and controls, and made the obvious suggestion that the maintenance contractors should be asked to inspect it carefully. He told his constable to take a few photographs, and then asked to interview Norman Poynter in his bedroom. When he met Norman, he made little effort to hide his conviction that anyone over the age of retirement was on the verge of senile dementia.

"Now let's go through this again, Mr Poynter," he said eventually. "I've seen the mess around and in the pool, but you maintain you didn't notice it immediately you came through the door. I don't understand that."

"You asked me for my first impression. It was the overpowering smell of chlorine."

"Then you became aware of the mess, and tripped over your dressing-gown and fell into the pool."

"Yes." Norman sighed; he was getting tired of this stupid policeman.

"I see," said Donaldson. "But I still don't understand, sir, what you were doing in the pool area, as you call it, so early in the morning." The Sergeant sounded as if he had scored a point.

Norman took a deep breath. His normally red face had grown brick-coloured, and Hugh Cassidy decided it was time to intervene before he had a stroke.

"Mr Poynter goes for a swim at that time almost every day," he said mildly.

"Ah!" said Donaldson but, after he and Dr Cassidy had left Norman's apartment, he added, "A funny old bloke, Dr Cassidy. You don't think he might have — "

"Caused the damage himself? Most certainly not!" Hugh was appalled at the suggestion.

"It was just a thought." Donaldson was not apologetic. "So have you any idea who it might have been? Not had any trouble like this before, have you?"

"No, to both questions," Hugh said shortly.

"Anyone around who's got a particular hate against you? Or reason to believe they have a grudge? What about these thefts you had? Staff, I assume. You sacked them?"

Thinking that Sergeant Donaldson was not an altogether stupid man, in spite of his self-satisfied air, Hugh considered the question. Their neighbour, Ashley Ormonde, certainly had no love of him or Evenlode, but it was impossible to imagine the dapper, not-so-young Ashley breaking into the pool area in the small hours, throwing the furniture around and the plants into the water and tampering with the chlorine metering equipment; he would have despised such behaviour as uncivilized. As for Zena Wilson and her mother, he doubted if either of them would have had the know-how to flood the pool with chlorine.

"Again — I can't help," he said, wording his answer carefully. "I'm not aware of having any personal enemies who would go in for mindless vandalism, and the girl who was sacked wouldn't have a clue about how to fix the chlorine."

"You mention 'mindless vandalism', Doctor." For a moment Donaldson was silent as if contemplating some great possibility. "Perhaps it was just that, inspired by Mr Balham's article in the *Colombury Courier*."

"Perhaps," Hugh agreed. "What are the chances that you'll catch the culprit or culprits, Sergeant?"

Donaldson shook his head. "If I'm to be honest, Doctor, the answer is 'none', but we'll do our best."

Seeing off the premises Sergeant Donaldson and the constable, who had made some notes but not uttered a word throughout the visit, Hugh felt despondent. There was a lot to be organized. The insurance would pay for the glass door that had been smashed, any furniture that had been damaged and the ruined plants, but the replacements would have to be purchased. The final job of making the pool once more safe and available could be left to the maintenance contractors, who would in any case, as Donaldson said, have to examine the chlorine pump, but the preliminary work would be laborious and dirty; he would have to help Simon and Patrick. And the sooner everything was done the better. The bright, warm sunny weather meant that the unavailability of one of the most popular meeting places for residents would be particularly annoying. He turned to the telephone.

★ ★ ★

By the time that Norman Poynter reappeared just before lunch, most of the residents were aware that the pool and the surrounding area had been vandalized and had heard of Norman's adventure. Everyone was shocked and disgusted about the pool and Norman found himself the centre of attention, which he rather enjoyed. "Washed and scrubbed and free of the stink of chlorine," as he put it, he was once more his old self and had recovered from the shock of the accident. Even his spectacles had been restored to him, unharmed.

Nevertheless, Norman's exploit completely eclipsed the news that Morag Luton's nephew was coming to dinner that evening, and the more improbable news that Mrs Dorothy Webb's sister had invited her to stay for a few days, and Dorothy would be off on Friday.

★ ★ ★

Not long before midnight Simon and Patrick fell into their respective beds. They were exhausted. Wearing old swimming trunks, they had set to work immediately after lunch, by which time an insurance adjuster had inspected the place, the smell of chlorine had largely dispersed and the water had been drained from the pool, leaving a detritus of mud and garden furniture and broken plants on the floor of the pool and its surround. It was filthy and tiring work, but at least the place was ready for the real cleaning to be done by the maintenance men in the morning. The two boys had refused Hugh's help.

Instead, at Simon's suggestion, having shown the insurance adjuster the state of the area and the extent of the damage, Hugh decided what replacements were needed, and drove into Colombury. The bar — with the liquor and glasses in a locker beneath it — had luckily not been touched, and the tables, chairs and loungers were made of hard and durable plastic and had suffered little. A good hosing down would restore them to their pristine state. However, all the cushions and umbrellas, which had been in the water, would be stained and useless, so that new ones would have to be bought.

Hugh dealt with this problem first. That done, he went to the local nursery, where he found a couple of dwarf trees, plants and new pots to replace those that were broken. To his surprise in both places, and at the glaziers, the news of the vandalism at Evenlode House was already known. As a result everyone was very sympathetic and, apart from the glaziers who had to order the glass for the sliding door, promised to deliver his purchases that afternoon.

By the end of the day, therefore, thanks to the cooperation Hugh had received in Colombury and the Trojan efforts of Simon and Patrick, the area, except for a boarded-up door and a lack of water in the pool, was back to normal. The three men regarded the scene with satisfaction.

"Now," Hugh said, "if the contractors come and do their stuff first thing, as they promised, and assure us that the chlorine metering system is in full working order, we'll fill the pool immediately, so that it can be used by the next day, if not tomorrow evening. You boys deserve medals."

"All I ask," said Patrick, "is just an hour alone with the jokers who made the damned mess. I'd happily drown them — in chlorinated water."

"And I'd help you," Simon said, swallowing a yawn. "We might even include Michael Balham if that Sergeant's right and it was his article that inspired the vandals."

Hugh laughed. "It'll be interesting to read what Balham has to say about the incident tomorrow. He hasn't been near Evenlode, but doubtless he'll concoct a piece."

* * *

Hugh was right. The next day's *Courier* contained a story by Michael Balham on the vandalism at Evenlode. It was reasonably sympathetic in tone; neither Balham nor the *Courier* approved of vandals. But again, considering that he hadn't been near the place, Balham showed a surprisingly detailed knowledge of what had occurred and the damage that had been done.

How, for instance, had he learnt that the bar had not been broken into and liquor stolen? Who had known this, Hugh wondered, apart from himself and Cindy, Simon and Patrick. The girls, Jill, Sarah and Val? They hadn't been near the pool and to his knowledge that particular subject hadn't come up in conversation; when questioned, both Simon and Patrick denied mentioning it to anyone; they had been busy and it simply hadn't occurred to them. Lucinda said the same, so none of the residents would have known either. That left Sergeant Donaldson and his silent constable, but they could hardly be suspected of telling tales out of school.

Hugh abandoned the conundrum; there was too much else to do.

8

"GOOD morning, Professor Luton."

"Hi, Miss Field! How are you? All right if I go straight up to Auntie's apartment?"

"Of course."

It was Friday morning. Sarah, her time divided between the reception desk and the office behind, was busy with a multitude of small chores. But it was part of her job to be pleasant to residents and their guests.

"Your letter has just come," she said, as Angus Luton seemed to linger. "Jill took it up to Mrs Luton."

"My letter?"

"Yes. The one you wrote your aunt from Canada saying you were coming to England and would be visiting her. At least, I assume that's what it said. Anyway, it was from you. It had a sticker with your name on it in the corner."

"And it only arrived this morning?

How — how absurd! Really too silly! The mails are impossible." Luton was frowning in exasperation. "I should have called Auntie from Ottawa before I left."

"Well, it no longer matters, does it?" Sarah said consolingly. "You're here now."

Her telephone started to burr and she excused herself. The caller was Mrs Grey. She had been unfortunately delayed and wouldn't be able to pick up Miss Webb, her sister, as she had arranged. Miss Webb, who was to stay with her for a few days, would have to come by bus. If someone from Evenlode would take her to the bus station in Colombury it wouldn't be inconvenient for her. The bus stopped at the end of the Greys' drive, so she wouldn't have a long walk.

Mrs Grey gave Sarah no opportunity to comment that it might not be inconvenient for the Greys or Miss Webb, but it was extremely inconvenient for the Evenlode staff. Someone would have to stop whatever they were doing and drive Dorothy into Colombury and put her on to her bus, for Miss Webb was apt to get flustered and was quite capable of getting on to the wrong bus, in which case the Cassidys would be blamed — at least by Mrs Grey.

"I see," Sarah replied. "I'll do my best to arrange it. Have you spoken to Miss Webb on her own line?"

"No, I haven't. I expected you to tell her when you'd got her organized."

"Yes, of course, Mrs Grey," said Sarah shortly.

But before Sarah could take any action about Dorothy Webb there were several interruptions. Norman Poynter wanted a parcel weighed and correctly stamped, Kenneth Barnard wanted to arrange for a couple of friends to come to dinner that evening and another resident had a loose tooth and wanted advice on a dentist. In between all this, the telephone rang twice.

Then, when Sarah was at last free to deal with the problem of Dorothy Webb and her transport, Angus Luton returned. He was full of apologies.

"I'm sorry to bother you," he said, "but I can't find Auntie. She's not in her apartment or anywhere around."

"Have you looked in the drawing-room — the pool area?"

"Yes. Of course, she could be somewhere in the garden. But I can't wait, Miss Field."

"But — but — I thought you were staying for the weekend, Professor. We've booked a guest room for you."

"I know. That's what I'd hoped to do, but alas I'll have to postpone the pleasure."

"Your aunt will be disappointed."

"I'm afraid so, but — " Luton leaned confidentially across the reception desk towards Sarah — "unfortunately things aren't going as I expected. To be candid, I don't think I can accept Oxford's offer, though I haven't completely given up hope. It's different at home. There I get room and board, but here . . . I'm afraid it's a question of money. Anyway, there's another chance of staying in England — I might be offered a fellowship at the London School of Economics — which is why I've got to go to London. I'll get in touch with Auntie from there as soon as I can."

"All right," Sarah said. "So, would

you like to leave your aunt a note? We've paper and envelopes right here, of course."

"No need," said Angus. "You'll be a dear, won't you, and explain to Auntie for me?"

"Very well. I'll do my best," Sarah said dubiously. "Anyway, I'm sorry about Oxford. Perhaps it will work out."

"Keep your fingers crossed."

"Yes," said Sarah, but she was distracted by the appearance of Dorothy Webb, who was looking both excited and anxious.

"I don't suppose my sister is here yet," she said. "I'm early. I've always been one of those people who are early for trains and planes and any sort of appointment."

"Miss Webb — " Sarah began. The thought had crossed her mind that perhaps Angus Luton would be prepared to take Dorothy Webb into Colombury and see her on to her bus, but he was already disappearing through the front door. "Miss Webb, your sister has phoned to say that unfortunately she can't come to fetch you, but — "

"Then how am I to get there? It was to

be such a treat. The Greys live so — so elegantly, and I was looking forward to — to a few days with them, and now you tell me . . . Oh dear!" Miss Webb put down the suitcase she was carrying and looked desperately about her. "What am I to do?"

"Can I help?"

"Mrs Horne!" Sarah smiled her relief; Mrs Horne was never a nuisance. "It's no great crisis. I was about to explain to Miss Webb that her sister can't come for her, but someone will put her on the bus in Colombury and — "

"Perhaps I could do that," Anne Horne volunteered. "I'm going to the hairdresser's and it would be no bother."

"Are you sure, Mrs Horne? We don't want to impose." Sarah was pleased at this solution, but hesitant.

"Quite sure, my dear Sarah. I'm so grateful that I can still drive competently at my age that I'm glad to give anyone a lift — and of course Dorothy is more than welcome." She picked up Dorothy's suitcase. "Come along," she said. "There's no problem."

★ ★ ★

On his way downstairs in search of a drink before lunch Kenneth Barnard went along to Morag Luton's apartment to return a book she had lent him. He rang the bell, but there was no answer, and he was about to turn away when he thought he heard voices. He rang again without result, and then opened the letter-box and listened. At once he recognized the voice of a BBC announcer, and smiled broadly to himself; Morag had gone out and left her radio on.

If he had not happened to meet Jill as he went into the drawing-room Kenneth would probably not have bothered to mention the matter to anyone; it was of singularly small importance. However, when Jill stopped him to ask if either of his guests that evening was on a diet or had any particular food allergies, he remarked, "Incidentally, I don't know where Mrs Luton is, but she doesn't seem to be at home and she's left her radio on."

"Oh dear!" Jill said. "I'll go and turn it off for her."

Minutes later, white-faced, Jill burst into the kitchen. Her mother, with the help of Val and the daily staff, was cooking the residents' lunch and making advance preparations for dinner. Her father and Simon were having a quick sandwich, which was all they allowed themselves in the middle of the day.

Mindful that there were more than family present, Jill made an effort to control her voice. "Dad, would you come, please. Mrs Luton is — unwell."

But once outside the kitchen door she seized Hugh by the arm. "Dad, she's dead! Morag Luton's dead!"

"What? Are you sure, Jill?"

Jill nodded. Although she had trained to be a nurse it had been a shock, first to realize that Morag was in the room, then that she was cold with no pulse. She had taken Morag her breakfast earlier that morning and the old lady had been her usual bright, birdlike self. Now . . .

"I'll get my bag from the office," Hugh said grimly. "You'd better come with me, Jill. Let's hope you're wrong and she's just collapsed."

It was a vain hope. Only the briefest

examination was needed to convince Hugh Cassidy that Morag Luton was indeed dead, and had been dead for some hours. Slowly he straightened himself and looked down sadly at the small frail body. She had been one of the first residents to come to Evenlode and, in his opinion, was one of the pleasantest. He felt personal grief at her death, but it was over-ridden by the realization of what this fresh misfortune would mean to Evenlode, and the practical difficulties it would cause.

"What was it, Dad? Heart?"

"Probably, Jill. The post-mortem should show."

"There'll have to be a PM?"

"I assume so, and possibly an inquest. Mrs Luton was seventy-one, but she was in excellent health and, though in a sense she was under my general care, I never actually treated her for anything. She wasn't even a victim of the food poisoning outbreak we had the other week."

"I see. All the same, it won't be very good publicity for us, will it? Not after all our other troubles."

Hugh shook his head. "No. Doubtless Mr Balham will make the worst he can of it, and there'll be other problems. But we can't stand around talking, Jill. You go and break the news to the family, but tell them to keep it quiet. I'll phone Dr Band, and get him to come and give a second opinion, just to cover myself. Luckily he's not only the local police doctor, but a sensible man. Then I'll have to notify the coroner's office, I suppose, and get in touch with Mrs Luton's solicitor. His name's Crewe, I think. It's on her file."

"What about the nephew, Professor Luton? We aren't expecting him now, are we?"

"No. Ask Sarah if she knows how to get hold of him."

* * *

"Dead?" Sarah was appalled.

"Keep your voice down," Jill urged as some of the residents walked across the hall to the dining-room.

"When? How? Did she have an accident?"

Jill shook her head. "Probably heart. Some hours ago. Listen, if anyone asks where she is, say she's unwell and staying in her room. Meanwhile we must try to contact her nephew."

"He's gone to London. Oh, Jill, she must have been there when he rang her bell. After all, she was expecting him. Perhaps she was no more than feeling ill, but couldn't answer. If I'd got someone to check on her at once she might have been saved."

"Nonsense! It must have been over very quickly. She didn't even have time to press her panic button, though that's what it's for. We can't check whenever someone doesn't answer his or her doorbell, so for heaven's sake don't blame yourself."

"No." Sarah knew that what Jill was saying was true, but . . .

"Did the Professor leave an address in London?"

"No, though he did mention something about LSE. He just said he'd be in touch."

"Right. I'll tell Dad. At least we won't have to bother with a sorrowing relation immediately, which is something to be thankful for." Jill stopped abruptly as Anne Horne came through the front door and approached the reception desk. "Hello, Mrs Horne," she said. "You do look nice. You've been to the beauty salon."

"Thank you. I'm glad you think it's an improvement."

Jill flushed. Mrs Horne was not usually so tart. "I must go," she said and, giving Sarah a warning glance, hurriedly excused herself.

Anne Horne looked after her with some amusement, tinged with regret. She was sorry she had spoken so sharply, but she was not in the best of tempers. Things had not gone well that morning. She never enjoyed the time spent — or wasted as she felt — under the uncomfortable hair-drier, or the feel of the arthritic hands being manipulated by the manicurist.

What was more, today her usual girl had been off duty and the substitute had been rough. Anne was not, and never had been, a vain woman, but she disliked the outward signs of old age, and did her best to forestall them.

She turned to Sarah. "I thought I should let you know that I put Miss Webb on to her bus safely."

"Thank you. It was awfully good of you to offer." Sarah wrenched her thoughts away from Morag Luton. "I hope it wasn't a bother."

"Not a bit," Anne Horne lied.

In fact, Dorothy Webb had been more trying than usual, or so she had seemed. She had kept on and on, worrying about her clothes, whether she had packed the most suitable garments, worrying if the seam of the dress she had mended had been well enough done since, with her poor eyesight, she had had to borrow a needle-threader before she could even thread her needle, worrying about missing the bus. Anne had been glad to say goodbye to her.

"Well, that's great. Thank you again, Mrs Horne," Sarah said.

She forced herself to smile and, as Anne Horne went off to her apartment, returned her thoughts to Morag Luton. If Mrs Luton's death had been a shock to her, she realized, it would be far more of a shock to Morag Luton's friends among the residents, and to her nephew, Angus Luton. And how, she wondered, would it affect the Cassidys and Evenlode.

★ ★ ★

Very shortly after one o'clock Dr Band was having a drink with Hugh Cassidy in the Cassidy's apartment. Dick Band was sixty and seriously considering retirement, but he still found his occasional police work intriguing and was loath to give up his connection with the Thames Valley Force.

Now he sat back comfortably in his armchair, legs crossed, and, smoothing a hand over his completely bald head — an unconscious mannerism when he was thinking — regarded Hugh quizzically. He had given Morag Luton's body a brief examination, inspected the apartment and noted that Mrs Luton had been almost within reach of her panic button when she died. But his naturally suspicious mind had noticed nothing out of order.

"What's the problem, Hugh?" he asked.

Band had known Hugh Cassidy before

the Cassidys had come to Evenlode House. Indeed, Hugh had consulted him about its possibilities and he had advised strongly against the undertaking, pointing out that they would be putting all their eggs in one basket with a vengeance. Nevertheless, he had to admit that, his advice ignored, the Cassidys had made a success of Evenlode and the place had prospered and gained an excellent reputation.

"You read the *Courier*, Dick." It was a statement rather than a question.

"Mr Balham's pieces? Of course."

"Then you've some idea of what's been happening here. We've had a succession of unpleasant and unfortunate incidents that could have ruined the whole atmosphere of Evenlode. And now poor Morag Luton — "

"Well, no one can blame you for that, Hugh — not even Balham."

"Oh yes, he can. He'll emphasize the long time-gap between her presumed death and when she was found, and the fact that the panic button wasn't within her reach. He has a damnably cunning knack of twisting facts, and he isn't helping to make Evenlode popular."

"You could always try suing him and the *Courier*."

"What for? You know as well as I do that I haven't got a case and, even if I had, I couldn't afford it," said Hugh bitterly, and thought that Morag Luton's death was going to cause financial problems, as well as everything else. "Anyway, what really worries me is the other residents. I'm afraid Mrs Luton's death will be a dreadful shock to them, especially those with whom she was friendly."

"For heaven's sake, Hugh! Why should it be such a shock? Mrs Luton may be the first but she won't be the last to die at Evenlode. Your residents are all over seventy. They've made it to three score and ten. They can't expect to live for ever."

Hugh made a gesture of annoyance. "You're as bad as that Sergeant Donaldson, Dick. The residents here are not fools, nor are they geriatric. With the possible exception of Miss Webb, they've all led comfortable lives. They've never experienced want. They've never suffered any physical hardship. They've always had the best of private medicine, dentistry, ophthalmology and, although all this is no guarantee of longevity, as we both know, it does help enormously. They may be in their seventies but they expect to live into their eighties. They don't feel they have one foot in the grave, not yet. Most of them still drive a car. They go away for holidays with family — if they're lucky enough to have any — or friends. They go to London on shopping sprees. They — " Hugh stopped, shaking his head in exasperation.

"OK, Hugh." Dick Band laughed. "That was quite a speech and you've made your point. Your residents may not be in the first bloom of youth, but they live the life of Riley. Why not? I don't begrudge it them, as Michael Balham seems to. And, of course, you're right," he added, suddenly serious. "The death of someone you know is, to a greater or lesser extent, a shock, even if it's expected — and when it happens out of the blue, it can be a great blow."

"Fair enough," said Hugh. "But let's ask ourselves seriously if I can sign a death certificate. Don't forget that Mrs Luton was not under my direct care at the time of her death. In fact, as far as I could tell, she was hale and hearty. Would you sign a certificate, in these circumstances? What can one say as cause of death, for instance?"

"I see what you mean," said Band thoughtfully. "No, I wouldn't, and I guess the coroner would demand a PM, in any case."

★ ★ ★

Hugh Cassidy came into the dining-room at the end of luncheon, and made a brief announcement. He said that Morag Luton had died suddenly that morning; the cause of death was not known at the moment, but it had clearly been quick and painless. This opinion had been confirmed by Dr Dick Band, whom he had called in. The coroner and Mrs Luton's solicitor had both been informed, and Mrs Luton's body would be taken to Oxford during the afternoon. He would let them know in due course when and where the funeral was to take place.

The announcement was received in stunned silence, followed by a babble of conversation.

"Poor little Morag!" exclaimed Kenneth Barnard.

"We shall miss her," said Norman Poynter.

"Yes. She was a dear," said Melissa Sarson.

Anne Horne nodded her agreement. She too would miss Morag Luton. She was surprised at how upset she felt. It was only later in the day that she realized she had been thinking not just of Morag, but of the effect her death might have on the Cassidys and everyone at Evenlode.

The Second Letter

Evenlode House,
Evenlode,
Oxfordshire.
July 5th 199-

MY dear Dick,
Many thanks for your letter, or perhaps I should thank Hilary. I rather suspect she wrote it and you just signed it. Anyway, it was good to get your news and know that all is going well with you.

I'm sorry you're unable to come for a weekend at present, but I appreciate how busy you must be and, of course, what little free time you have you want to spend with Hilary and young Peter. And I have to admit, though the offer stands, that it's probably a good idea to postpone a visit.

Evenlode is not a very happy place at the moment. You may have read about some of our woes. The local paper made *a big thing of them, but they've received wider coverage than that. They were reported briefly in the London dailies, and a friend in Yorkshire phoned to ask if I was all right! Needless to say, the reporting was full of inaccuracies.*

Anne Horne went on to recount the various incidents that had recently bedevilled Evenlode House, and Chief Inspector Richard Tansey, reading the succinct and informative account, wished that all his underlings at the Thames Valley Police HQ could prepare such excellent material. The letter continued:

I find it difficult to believe that these various incidents are coincidental, but there would seem to be no other explanation, and what seriously worries me is their cumulative effect. They could, with the unexpected death of Morag Luton this morning, spell the end of Evenlode House, at least as the wonderful haven it was until recently.
The terms on which residents live here are extremely complicated, but I wasn't married to John for fifty years

without learning something about legal matters, and his former partners gave me excellent advice before I signed the agreement. To simplify, residents buy a leasehold on their apartments of fifteen years or for life, whichever is the longer, so that they have complete security, though their equity decreases each year. After fifteen years the apartment is worth nothing to their estate, but reverts to the Cassidys, though of course they can go on living here until they die. However, should death occur before the end of the fifteen years, the Cassidys have to buy back whatever part of the lease is outstanding, which in Morag's case will mean producing a considerable sum of money. I very much doubt if they have it.

I suppose it was a gamble on the Cassidys' part that none of us would die so soon or, if someone did, that they would be able to re-sell very quickly. And they may well have lost the gamble, because after all the adverse publicity Evenlode has been getting it won't be so easy to find another resident to replace Morag. This may well mean they will have to sell the place and, even if the residents are not bought out, Evenlode will never be the same without the Cassidys. Of course, this was the gamble we had to take, and it looks as if we too may have lost. So much for security.

But why should I bother you with all this? My pen has run away with me as it often does these days, and maybe I'm being over-pessimistic.

With every best wish, and my love to you and Hilary and Peter,

Your affectionate aunt,
Anne.

On Monday morning Dick Tansey passed the letter across the breakfast table to his wife, and shook his head sadly. "Poor old dear," he said. "She really does sound depressed. I'll have to make an effort to go and visit her."

9

DR BAND was right. A post-mortem was judged essential to establish the cause of death. But the pathologist considered it to be a mere formality and, on the same Monday morning that Tansey received his letter from Mrs Horne, Dr Ghent assigned the task to one of his juniors. Because he was a junior, and because this was the first PM he had performed without supervision, he was excessively thorough, and it was with eyes shining and cheeks red with excitement that he went to report to Ghent.

"She was murdered!" he said triumphantly. "That cadaver — Mrs Luton — was murdered!"

At first, Ghent greeted this announcement with cynical amusement, but his grin faded as the young man produced the evidence for his unexpected conclusion. He was right. It seemed that Morag Luton had almost certainly been suffocated by having some soft object — a cushion, probably, or a pillow — pressed over her face. Further confirmatory tests would be necessary, but the fibre in her lungs — which at first sight appeared to be wool — put the matter beyond reasonable doubt. The fact that the body had shown no signs of a struggle, which might have alerted Hugh Cassidy or, more likely, Dr Band, was explained by Morag Luton's small, birdlike frame. Even against a girl of average strength she would not have been able to offer much resistance, especially if she had been taken by surprise.

The information was passed on by phone to the coroner and Philip Midvale, the Chief Constable, with the promise of a full report the next day. Midvale did not receive the news with any pleasure. The Thames Valley Police Serious Crime Squad was at the moment under-manned and over-stretched, but by chance he himself had a cousin who was debating how to deal with a lonely widowhood, and he was not wholly unaware of the recent problems of Evenlode.

Pushing himself out of his custom-built

chair with some difficulty — for Midvale was a heavy man — the Chief Constable turned on his personal computer terminal and prodded at the keyboard. He might have been a general pondering his battle strategy, and to some extent he was. The computer, which was automatically updated, showed him the disposition of his forces — particularly on what cases his senior officers were employed, and gave the names of those sick or on leave. His resources were rarely enough for the tasks in hand, and today was no exception.

However, he noted with relief that Detective Chief Inspector Tansey of the Serious Crime Squad had just successfully secured a conviction in a case of armed robbery, and was at present dealing with a backlog of paperwork. He liked Tansey, and respected him, because time and time again the Chief Inspector had proved himself to be an intelligent, sensitive and resourceful officer. The paperwork would have to wait. Midvale poked his head into his secretary's office and told her to send for Tansey.

"Sit down, Chief Inspector," he said

when Tansey, a tall, lean rather elegant man, appeared, "and tell me if you've ever heard of a place called Evenlode House in the Cotswolds."

"Evenlode House?" Tansey was startled. "Yes, I know of it, sir. It's a kind of apartment hotel for rich elderly folk. It's near Colombury. I have an aunt who lives there, a Mrs Anne Horne. Actually she's not really my aunt, though I call her that. She's an old friend of my family."

"Well, I'm glad your aunt's not a Mrs Morag Luton, Tansey, because Mrs Luton, who also lives at Evenlode House, has been murdered — or at least it's a death we'll have to treat as a murder inquiry. I've not had the full report yet, but according to the PM she was smothered, probably with a cushion."

Tansey nodded dumbly. He was thinking of the letter from Anne Horne he had received that morning. There had been nothing in it to suggest that Morag Luton's death had been other than natural, but if that had been a blow to the owners and residents of Evenlode, the scandal of murder — if murder it was — would be a double blow, most likely a knock-out, coming on top of the other incidents Anne Horne had outlined.

" . . . I hope Mrs Horne's presence won't be an embarrassment to you, Chief Inspector, but there's no one else available at the moment, and the case shouldn't prove too difficult." The Chief Constable went on to brief Tansey on what he had been told, and concluded, "When elderly ladies get murdered it's usually for their money. But I mustn't prejudice you."

"No, indeed, sir." Tansey grinned, but he was remembering the last time the Chief Constable had handed him a supposedly simple case; he had ended up in hospital with a bullet in his shoulder.

★ ★ ★

Back in his own office, Tansey decided that it was too late to go out to Evenlode that day. Nor was there any pressing need. Morag Luton had apparently been killed on Friday morning, and it was now Tuesday. If anyone had wanted to destroy evidence in Mrs Luton's apartment there would have been plenty of opportunity.

142

And in these circumstances it could only be beneficial, Tansey knew, to do some homework before he approached the case.

He arranged that Bill Abbot, a detective-sergeant, whom he liked and with whom he had often worked before, should pick him up at home the following morning at eight. Then, . after some telephoning, including a call to Dr Band, who received his news about Morag Luton with surprise and assured him that there had been nothing in her apartment to hint at foul play, he drove himself from the Kidlington Headquarters into Oxford.

Dr Ghent, the pathologist, greeted him pleasantly, if without enthusiasm, and escorted him down to the cold formaldehyde-smelling morgue, where an attendant pulled out a metal tray and drew down a sheet to reveal Morag Luton's body. In death she looked even smaller and more birdlike than when she had been alive.

"She put up no resistance?" Tansey asked.

"No," said Ghent, and added surprisingly, "Poor little thing! She wouldn't

143

have had a chance, even against a small boy."

Tansey nodded. There were no small boys at Evenlode. But could the strength of a small boy equate with that of an old man, perhaps in a sudden fit of rage? Recalling the Chief Constable's comment that elderly ladies were usually murdered for their money, Tansey reminded himself that there could be other reasons. He indicated to Ghent that he had seen enough and the two men left the morgue.

"You'll get a full report in the morning, Chief Inspector," Ghent said as Tansey was leaving.

"Yes. Many thanks," said Tansey, and meant it; he believed that the more he knew about the victim the more likely he was to find the killer.

From one morgue, he went to another of a different kind. The office of the *Oxford Mail* also contained a file of the more recent back issues of the *Colombury Courier*, as well as the national press, and Tansey spent a good hour reading all he could about what Anne Horne had called the 'woes of Evenlode'. By the time he

144

reached home that night, he thought he had gained some greater awareness of the atmosphere of the place and the nature of its residents.

★ ★ ★

Sergeant Abbot arrived at the Tanseys' house at ten minutes to eight the next morning, but the Chief Inspector was ready and waiting for him. They drove in companionable silence until they were on the motorway, when Tansey said, "You're a local, Abbot, you were born and brought up in Colombury. What do you know about Evenlode House?"

"Next to nothing, sir," said Bill Abbot. "Evenlode itself is a pretty little village — not more than a dozen cottages, a church and a pub. The few big places are on the far side. As for this Evenlode House, it's way after my time and way out of my league. I gather it's some kind of retirement home for millionaires."

"That's an exaggeration," said Tansey, "but the residents certainly aren't on the breadline."

"I do know that the place is run by

some people called Cassidy; the man is a medical doctor," continued Abbot. "And I'll say this for them — they seem to buy most of their food and suchlike locally in Colombury or in Oxford. They're not like some, who get everything sent down from London. For instance, there's a neighbour of the Cassidys, called Ashley Ormonde, who wouldn't buy a bootlace locally if he could avoid it."

Tansey laughed. "The Cassidys are popular in the neighbourhood, then?"

"Yes, I would think so, sir."

But Sergeant Donaldson, the officer in charge of Colombury police station, on whom, duty-bound, they called, did not agree. "I wouldn't call them popular, sir," he said, challenging Abbot's opinion, "and I should know. It's my patch."

"Yes." Tansey avoided Abbot's eye. "The local paper doesn't seem to like them much, certainly," he said.

"Ah, that's Mr Balham. A clever young man, that," said Donaldson. "You'll be meeting him before long, I'll be bound, sir. As soon as he hears we suspect Mrs Luton's death wasn't natural and there's

146

a Chief Inspector on the case, he'll be after you."

"And I wouldn't be surprised if Mr Balham isn't hearing the glad news this very second," said Abbot sourly as they drove out of Colombury; he had not liked Donaldson's manner, nor his obvious dismay that the Kidlington detectives were not about to invite him to accompany them to Evenlode. "I can just imagine the sergeant hurrying to the blower the moment he got rid of us."

"It doesn't matter, Abbot," Tansey said. "By now quite a few people must know or guess that there are 'suspicious circumstances' surrounding Mrs Luton's death."

Tansey had left it up to Dr Band whether he should inform his colleague, Dr Cassidy, that Morag Luton's death would be the subject of a murder investigation. It had seemed to him that there was little to be gained by insisting on secrecy. Once Cassidy had been told that a Detective Chief Inspector would be calling on him the next day, it would come as no surprise that something was amiss, and it wouldn't need a genius to associate that something with Morag Luton's death.

Anne Horne, whom Tansey had phoned from his home the previous evening to warn her that he would be coming to Evenlode in an official capacity, had immediately asked if his visit concerned Morag's death, and he hadn't denied it. But he had given no details, and she had not asked for any. It was sufficient that he had stressed that his call was private; he knew she would keep her own counsel, whatever her personal fears and worries. He thought of her with affection, as Abbot drove through the leafy Cotswold lanes, and hoped for her sake that Evenlode House and the Cassidys would survive.

★ ★ ★

To judge from the grim expression and worried frown on Dr Hugh Cassidy's craggy face, the chances of this survival appeared to Tansey unlikely. A young man who had introduced himself as Simon Cassidy had met the Chief Inspector and his sergeant in the hall of Evenlode and taken them to the Cassidys' apartment.

Hugh Cassidy had greeted them, and made no pretence of ignorance of the reason for their presence. "Dr Band phoned me," he said at once, "and it was grievous news. Bad enough that Mrs Luton should have died suddenly and alone, unable to call for help, but that you're suggesting that she was murdered — that someone deliberately killed the poor little woman . . . " He shook his head in helpless anger. "Why, for God's sake? Why? I can't conceive of any explanation."

"That, Dr Cassidy, is what we're here to discover," Tansey said, "and who."

"Yes, of course, and I assure you you'll get every assistance from me and my family."

"Thank you," Tansey said mildly.

But he was soon to learn that Hugh Cassidy, in spite of his emotional outburst, which he guessed was out of character, was essentially a practical man. He had made for the police a photocopy of what he called Mrs Luton's file. It contained essential information about her age, illnesses — she had had surprisingly few — date of her arrival at Evenlode and the name of the solicitor who was to be informed in the event of her death.

"Have you been in touch with this Mr Crewe, Doctor?" Tansey asked.

"Yes, but not since — since I heard from Dr Band."

"Do you know anything about her will?" Tansey passed the photocopies to Abbot. "There's no mention of any relations or next-of-kin here."

"Her only relation was a nephew — and then only by marriage — a Professor Angus Luton. Mrs Luton's husband had a much younger brother, and I gather Angus was his only child. He lives in Canada, but has been over here recently, partly on business and partly on holiday. I have no idea if he's her heir. All I can tell you is that her estate will be considerable. She was a rich woman."

Tansey nodded his understanding. "Now, the morning Mrs Luton died. Can you give me an outline of events — when she had breakfast, that sort of thing?"

"I'll do my best, Chief Inspector, but

I can only give you approximate times, and most of it will be hearsay."

"That doesn't matter at the moment," Tansey assured him, and listened carefully as Hugh Cassidy recounted what he knew. When he had finished, Tansey said, "I see. Dr Cassidy, you say your daughter found Mrs Luton dead. How did she know? Most people — "

"Jill trained as a nurse — she qualified, but didn't like it — so she had a pretty good idea, and when I examined Mrs Luton a very short time later I found her skin was cold, though there was no sign of any rigor mortis. At an estimate I'd say she'd been dead between one and three hours. I couldn't be more accurate. It was a warm day. Dr Band agreed with me. But of course you have more information from the pathologist by now."

"And I hope to get yet more, Dr Cassidy." Tansey grinned. He wanted Cassidy to relax; the man was very tense, but in the circumstances this was only to be expected. "Tell me more about this Professor — Mrs Luton's nephew — would you?"

Hugh shrugged. "I don't know much, though Mrs Luton loved to talk about him — she was proud of him and, as I said, he was her only relation. He was apparently a professor at some Canadian university over here to see about a job in Oxford."

"When did he first come to visit his aunt?"

"About ten days ago. The Saturday before last, to be precise. He telephoned Mrs Luton from Oxford. It was a complete surprise to her. He had written from Canada, but the letter hadn't arrived . . . "

Hugh Cassidy continued and Abbot took rapid notes, but the number of different names and their various relationships were beginning to irritate the Sergeant.

"Chief Inspector, sir," he said as Hugh paused. "May I suggest it would be a help if we could have the names and perhaps a little information about everyone living and working here. Dr Cassidy refers to 'the family', but I'm not clear — "

"Of course. How stupid of me," said

Cassidy. "I should have thought of that before. I'll get Sarah to prepare it. Everything's in the computer. It won't take long."

"Splendid!" said Tansey, blessing Sergeant Abbot; he had been wondering if Sarah was another married daughter. "Perhaps while she's doing that we might have a look at Mrs Luton's apartment. Has it been cleaned since Saturday?"

"Why, yes." Hugh Cassidy gritted his teeth. "I'm sorry, Chief Inspector. It never occurred to us. Why should it? We didn't know then that it might be a case of murder," he concluded sadly.

10

THE first question Tansey asked when they entered Morag Luton's apartment was, "Where exactly was the body found, Dr Cassidy?"

"Right here, on this sofa, when I reached her, and I'm sure Jill hadn't moved her," replied Cassidy.

Then Tansey saw the cushion. There were others, but they were covered in velvet, and the fibres in Morag's lungs had been of wool. This cushion, the suspect, was needle-work, a posy of flowers cross-stitched in wool of various colours on a beige background. It was, Tansey supposed, very pretty, but he regarded it with some distaste.

"We'll need a large plastic bag, Sergeant."

"Yes, sir. There are a couple in the car. Shall I fetch them now?"

"Please," said Tansey.

"What do you want a bag for?" Hugh Cassidy was puzzled.

"For that cushion," Tansey pointed. "It could well have been the weapon."

"Oh God!" Hugh winced, imagining the scene.

Tansey picked up a large studio portrait of a young man. "This is Mrs Luton's nephew, the professor from Canada?"

"Yes. That's quite a good likeness, though a bit flattering, and taken a few years ago, I believe. But he seemed a very pleasant chap."

Tansey regarded the photograph thoughtfully. A simple case, the Chief Constable had remarked, and indeed it did seem likely to be so. Nephew pays aunt a flying visit, ingratiates himself with the Evenlode household, murders her and has sudden urgent business elsewhere, only to be surprised when he telephones in a week or two to learn that the old girl is dead and he has inherited a fortune! That this was a conceivable explanation of Morag Luton's death, Tansey was perfectly aware; many criminals, both professional and amateur, were amazingly stupid at times. But somehow he couldn't believe that this was such a case. Could a professor really be so unsophisticated? And what about Evenlode's other misfortunes? Were they totally irrelevant?

While he ruminated Tansey was inspecting the contents of the drawers of an escritoire — postage stamps, a card offering a dental appointment, a letter of thanks from someone who sounded like an old servant, a bill from Harrods, out of date theatre programmes, a book catalogue and an envelope containing snapshots of Angus Luton.

"I'd like to take this envelope, Dr Cassidy, and the studio portrait of Professor Luton," Tansey said on the spur of the moment. "We'll give you receipts for them and the cushion before we go. All right?"

Hugh Cassidy nodded; he didn't ask why the police might want the snaps. Abbot had returned and was carefully putting the needlework cushion into its plastic bag. Tansey led the way into the bedroom, but they found nothing interesting there.

"Dr Cassidy, you mentioned that your daughter used a pass key to get into the apartment. How many such master keys would there be, and who would have them?"

"I always keep one with me, and so do Simon and Patrick, my son-in-law. Then there are three in the office, which the staff borrow and return as soon as they're finished with them; that's a strict rule. Then there's a spare one in my wife's and my bedroom just in case of an emergency in the middle of the night. That makes seven. But remember, Chief Inspector, Mrs Luton would have opened her door to anyone who rang the bell, especially as she was expecting her nephew. It wouldn't have occurred to her to do otherwise." Hugh shook his head in disgust. "This is — or was — assumed to be a safe place."

"So what are the chances of a stranger just walking in last Friday, going up the stairs or using the lift and ringing that doorbell?"

"Five hundred to one against! Sarah was on duty at the reception desk in the hall throughout the morning, my wife and other staff were in the back premises, and there were a lot of residents moving around the building, so it would have taken some nerve to walk in as you suggest. Besides, if you're thinking of a sneak thief, Chief Inspector, nothing was taken. There was a hundred pounds in Mrs Luton's wallet and it wasn't touched."

If Hugh Cassidy realized that he had narrowed the field of potential suspects he gave no sign of it. "What would you like to do next, Chief Inspector?" he asked, smiling wryly. "Question people, I suppose."

"I'm afraid so. I'd like to start with meeting what you call 'the family', and then at least a few of the residents — those most friendly with Mrs Luton, perhaps. Is there a room where we could hold interviews?"

"Yes. There's a small sitting-room which isn't much used. We could rearrange the furniture and plug in a phone. Perhaps you'd wait in the office while this is being organized. Sarah should have that list of Evenlode occupants ready by now. It will give you some idea of the set-up here, and she can explain anything that isn't clear. Then later you might like to look around the place."

"Thank you. That will be great," said Tansey. "We appreciate your cooperation and we'll do our best to inconvenience everyone as little as possible. Unfortunately, we're bound to disturb the smooth running of your establishment to some extent. For example, there will be a scene of crime team here shortly to search this apartment thoroughly."

He paused, and then added, "Incidentally, Dr Cassidy, I think I should tell you that I'm not completely unfamiliar with Evenlode, though I've never been here before. One of your residents, Mrs Horne, is an old friend of my family, and we correspond. In fact, I had been intending to pay her a visit myself."

"Really? What a coincidence!" Hugh Cassidy sounded vaguely amused, and the information didn't seem to worry him, or even surprise him greatly. He gave Tansey one curious glance, but asked no questions. "I'll show you and Sergeant Abbot to the office right now," he said.

Sarah Field, Miss Field, according to the list — or rather lists — she had provided for the Chief Inspector, with duplicates for his sergeant, was obviously efficient. The residents' names were given in alphabetical order with the dates of their arrival at Evenlode and their apartment numbers. A second list gave the apartment numbers first, so that it was clear who were neighbours, and asterisks against certain names denoted those who, in Sarah's judgement, had been particularly friendly with Mrs Luton. Tansey was not surprised to see that one of these asterisked names was Anne Horne.

The third list was the most interesting to Tansey, once he had excluded the domestic and outdoor help. It explained what the Cassidys called 'the family' and their relationship to each other. Against her own name, Sarah had typed 'Old school friend of Jill'. Valerie Rowan was explained briefly as 'Friend of Simon'. With the exception of Miss Rowan, they were all listed as shareholders of Evenlode House.

"Thank you very much," Tansey said as Sarah reappeared to tell them that their interview room was ready and midmorning coffee would be waiting for them. "Perhaps if you'll lead the way, we can talk to you first," he suggested.

"Yes, of course."

The room, while it still failed to look entirely businesslike — certainly it remained more comfortable than a police interview room — had been sensibly adapted. There was a desk with a telephone, and an upright but comfortable chair for Tansey. To one side was a smaller table and a similar chair for Abbot. There were more such chairs for those to be questioned, and another table by a wall on which stood a tray of coffee and biscuits and a carafe of water with glasses.

"This is splendid," Tansey exclaimed.

"Good."

Without being asked, Sarah poured coffee and passed sugar and biscuits, then seated herself on a chair in front of the desk. She was pale but composed, a pleasant girl with an interesting rather than pretty face, Tansey thought, and clearly competent.

"You've known the Cassidys a long time, Miss Field," he said, opening the conversation on a casual note.

"Yes. My parents were killed in a car crash when I was at school — with Jill. My legal guardian wasn't really interested, and the Cassidys became a substitute family for me."

"So you're an adopted daughter, as it were."

It wasn't a question, and Sarah didn't attempt to answer it, but her mouth twisted into a sardonic expression which Tansey was unable to interpret. She said, "I act as receptionist cum accountant here, but we all muck in with whatever needs doing."

Rebuffed, Tansey took a different tack. Looking at the list in front of him, he said, "You comment that Miss Rowan is a friend of Simon Cassidy's. What does that mean exactly?"

"She's someone Simon met in Oxford and brought home a few weeks ago. She's still here." Sarah said coldly.

Tansey tried again. "Miss Field, how

162

good is your memory? What can you tell me about the Friday morning Mrs Luton died?"

"Was murdered," Sarah corrected him. "Or so Dr Cassidy told the family last night. But he said not to mention it to the residents," she added.

"I see," said Tansey. "That's fine. It's true we're treating this as a murder inquiry. Now, about that Friday morning?"

Sarah was young and she was intelligent. She explained lucidly. Professor Luton had said hello when he arrived about ten o'clock, and remarked how untrustworthy the mails — the post — was when she told him that a letter he had written to his aunt days ago from Canada had arrived that morning and been taken up to her room. That was about all. He had not mentioned his change of plans for the weekend until he had returned to the reception desk to say he couldn't find his aunt."

"Was he away long?" Tansey asked.

Sarah shrugged. "Ten minutes, perhaps. I was busy with phone calls. I couldn't really say."

"Did he seem agitated about his aunt?

Or was he eager to get away?"

Sarah gave Tansey a long, hard stare. "No, not as I recollect. He even told me why he couldn't stay for the weekend as he had expected. He had to see someone at the London School of Economics, where he now hoped he might get a Fellowship. The job that had been offered to him in Oxford had too many drawbacks — no free board or accommodation as he had at his Canadian university — and for financial reasons he didn't think he could accept it."

"Quite a long explanation." Tansey was thoughtful. "What about Mrs Luton? Did he ask to leave a note for her, or anything?"

"No. I offered him some paper and an envelope, but he refused them. He said he'd get in touch with her from London. In the meantime he asked me to explain."

"Curious," said Tansey. "Do you recall if he was carrying a weekend bag of any kind?"

"I'm sure he wasn't." Sarah was positive. "I remember looking after him as he went out of the door. It had crossed my mind that he might give one of the residents a lift into Colombury, but I hesitated to suggest it — and he'd gone. Anyway, he wouldn't have brought a bag in if he didn't intend to stay, would he?"

It was Tansey's turn to give Sarah a searching look. "Did you like Professor Luton, Miss Field?" he asked abruptly.

Sarah was nonplussed. "I scarcely knew him. I only met him twice, that Friday morning, and the Wednesday before when he came to dinner here."

"What about the first Saturday — the Saturday of the party Mrs Luton gave for him?"

"Dr Cassidy met him, and Val — Val Rowan — helped at the little party. He spent the evening here at Evenlode and I saw him, but I never spoke to him on that occasion."

"Nevertheless, you must have formed some opinion of him, Miss Field."

Sarah shrugged again. "If you want to know, I wasn't impressed. Give him a small moustache and he could have played the part of one of those spivs you

165

see in old 1950s' movies, the sort they show on television. But Mrs Luton was proud of him and, as I said, Val Rowan had more contact with him than I did, so her opinion should be worth more."

"We'll certainly ask her. Perhaps you'd be kind enough to send her along next."

"Yes. All right, as soon as I can find her. I expect she's somewhere with Simon." A shadow passed over her face, then she added, "Incidentally, Mrs Cassidy wants to know if you'd like to have lunch here."

"Please. It would be very convenient — save us driving into Colombury — but not if it's a bother."

"No bother. I'll tell her."

"Thank you, and thank you for answering our questions so clearly, Miss Field."

Sarah gave a little nod of her head in acknowledgement, and Abbot got up to open the door for her as she went, carrying the coffee tray. Shutting the door, he said, "A self-possessed young lady, sir. Somehow I don't think she likes Miss Rowan much."

Tansey grinned. "My opinion too,

166

Abbot. She didn't seem keen on Professor Luton either."

★ ★ ★

When Valerie Rowan came in both Tansey and Abbot were struck by the contrast between her and Sarah Field. What a pretty little piece, the sergeant thought, with her fair hair and big blue eyes, but as nervous as a kitten. The Chief Inspector's first impression was not identical. He thought she was a pretty girl, but far more ordinary than Sarah, and he was not attracted by her, though he could understand why Simon Cassidy might be. And this attraction might explain Sarah's reaction to the suggestion that she was an adopted daughter of the Cassidys, when perhaps she had hoped to be a daughter-in-law.

"Come and sit down, Miss Rowan," said the Chief Inspector.

"Oh, call me Val, please. Everyone does," she answered.

Tansey merely nodded. "You realize that this is an official police inquiry into the death of Mrs Morag Luton?"

"Yes, Chief Inspector, I do, and I'll answer any questions you like. It's a dreadful business. Mrs Luton was such a sweet old lady. In fact she didn't seem like an *old* lady. She was always bright and cheerful and she was very kind to me. That was a great help, because I've never before been a maid of all work, which is what I suppose I am here."

"So you needed people to be kind to you?" Tansey was amused.

"Yes, indeed. When I met Simon . . . Oh, that was so fortunate. The Cassidys have been so wonderful. I can't tell you."

But she did. There poured out of her the story of how she had met Simon, what straits she had been in at the time and how happy she was at Evenlode. "I'd do anything for the Cassidys," she concluded. "I've no qualifications, and without them I'd be homeless and on the dole."

"Tell us about the morning Mrs Luton was killed," Tansey said.

Val shivered. "She was just as usual, happy because — because her nephew was coming for the weekend. She was up when I came in about nine-fifteen. I made her bed and cleaned the bath and dusted a bit, though it wasn't really necessary."

"How long were you in the apartment?"

"Fifteen minutes, perhaps — no more."

"Did anyone ring the doorbell while you were there?"

"No." Val shook her head.

"What about the post?"

The question appeared to disturb her. "I — I don't know what you mean."

"Mrs Luton had a letter that morning. Did you deliver it?"

"No, and I don't know who did. It would have been put through her letter-box, but I didn't see it."

"You didn't notice an air mail envelope with a Canadian stamp anywhere while you were cleaning up?"

"No, I didn't."

"Right, Miss Rowan." Tansey seemed to have forgotten that he had been asked to call her Val. "The Saturday before all this, Mrs Luton gave a small party for her nephew. I'm told you helped."

"Yes. I poured drinks and passed canapés around."

"So you met Professor Luton."

"Yes. I arrived before the guests and was introduced to him. He was very nice and friendly, though he must be awfully clever to be a professor."

She had volunteered her opinion of Angus Luton — so different from Sarah Field's — without being asked, and Tansey said there were no more questions at the moment, but would she ask Mrs Donne to come in.

★ ★ ★

Jill Donne appeared more worried than nervous. She corroborated her father's account of how she had found Mrs Luton's body and had gone at once to fetch him. She agreed that it had been a shock; naturally she had seen dead bodies before when she had worked in a hospital, but then the deaths had usually been more or less expected. Mrs Luton had been so bright and chirpy, like a sparrow, she said, just a few hours before when she had taken her breakfast in at eight o'clock. It was difficult to believe that anyone had killed her.

"Did you notice anything unusual about the apartment, either at eight or when you found the body?" Tansey asked.

"No. At eight, I merely put her tray in its usual place. Then, later, I was only in the sitting-room a couple of minutes, and perhaps another five with Dad. There was nothing we could do for her. Or do you mean when I cleaned it on Sunday? I'm sorry about that, Chief Inspector, but it seemed a good idea as we weren't too busy. Mother and I gave it a good turnout, and later Simon checked the inventory. We didn't touch her personal belongings; we thought we should wait till we heard from her solicitor."

"Don't worry about it, Mrs Donne. I don't believe you destroyed any vital evidence, though our men will go over the apartment again. By the way, I suppose you didn't notice a letter with Canadian stamps on it lying around, did you?"

"The one from Professor Luton. I put it through Mrs Luton's letter-box around nine. She might have read it, then thrown it in her waste-paper basket as she wouldn't have been expected to answer it. In which case I'm afraid it's gone.

"It doesn't matter," Tansey said. "Did you ever meet Professor Luton?"

"I was introduced to him and we shook hands the first day he came, and we smiled at each other on the Wednesday." Jill shrugged. "That's all. I didn't see him at all the last Friday. He seemed friendly enough."

★ ★ ★

In the next hour the Chief Inspector questioned Mrs Cassidy, Simon and Patrick Donne, but learnt nothing further of importance. They all expressed anger and concern at Mrs Luton's death. They had had almost no contact with her nephew, apart from the most casual pleasantries, and had formed no particular opinion of him. Nevertheless, said Simon, he considered Angus Luton the prime suspect, and Patrick, even more blunt, said that for Angus Luton to be guilty would be the best solution for Evenlode House. Obviously the two young men had discussed the situation.

But it was Lucinda Cassidy who made the most astute comment. She said, "Chief Inspector, Evenlode is an unusual place, a friendly place, but there is a divide between the residents and 'the family' — as everyone calls it — a divide which both sides respect. You'll find out considerably more about Morag Luton and her nephew from her friends among the residents than from us."

11

"THAT'S the best meal I've had in a long time," said Sergeant Abbot, finishing his tankard of beer and wiping his mouth. "You know, sir, when you told Miss Field we'd like to eat here and not go into Colombury I thought regretfully of the Windrush Arms and my usual pint, but after this . . . " He shook his head slowly.

Tansey laughed. "You're putting on weight, Abbot."

Abbot patted his stomach. "Yes, I'm afraid I am. My wife's a jolly good cook too, but not in Mrs Cassidy's league. They're nice people, the Cassidys, aren't they, sir?"

"Yes, indeed. It'll be a shame if they have to give up Evenlode."

By common consent the two police officers had not discussed Morag Luton's death over their early lunch, which had been served to them in their room so that they could avoid any curious glances from the residents. But the meal now over, Abbot said, "I noticed you never asked anyone this morning about the various incidents that have happened here recently. You seemed to concentrate on the nephew. Did you have a reason, sir?"

"To be honest, Abbot, no. I was just fishing. I sense there must be some connection between the incidents, as we call them, and the death, but for the life of me I can't imagine what it might be. And anyway I could easily be wrong."

"Maybe."

Abbot had great faith in Detective Chief Inspector Tansey. Tansey could make mistakes but, if he did, he admitted them readily, and he was always prepared to acknowledge when he was at a loss. What was more, he never claimed someone else's brainchild as his own, but was generous in giving credit to others.

"Anyway, we'll get around to the unfortunate happenings eventually — if it proves necessary," Tansey continued. "First thing this afternoon one of the Cassidys is going to show us around

Evenlode so we'll have a better idea of the background, and be able to visualize all the events more easily. Then Dr Cassidy's going to take us to pay calls on a few of the residents who were friendly with Mrs Luton. And, you never can tell, Abbot," Tansey added, straight-faced, "we might even get offered tea and cakes!"

Before Abbot could think of a suitable retort, Simon Cassidy came into the room and said that if they were ready it would be an ideal time to look around, as the residents were now having their lunch. Simon, who knew they already had a general idea of the layout of Evenlode, took them to the long drawing-room with its bar at the end, then showed them the kitchen quarters, from which they could see through to the dining-room, and on to the pool area, where one of the sliding glass panels was still boarded up.

"We've had to order the glass, and it hasn't come yet," said Simon, gesturing towards the board. "You've heard about the place being vandalized, Chief Inspector?"

"Yes. That was bad luck."

"Luck had nothing to do with it, Chief

Inspector!" Simon corrected Tansey fiercely. "It was a result of definite provocation from that damned journalist, Michael Balham of the *Colombury Courier*. He more or less said that Evenlode was a racket, and shouldn't be allowed to exist."

"The place was left in a mess, was it?"

"A mess is an understatement. Furniture and plants were thrown into the pool and it was absolute chaos. Just wanton destruction!" Simon concluded in disgust.

"Any idea why this chap Balham should have such a down on Evenlode?" Tansey asked casually.

"He's a nasty piece of work, that's all I can tell you, and if poor Mr Poynter had been drowned that morning, he'd have been responsible."

From the pool area Simon led Tansey and Abbot outside, and showed them the garage block and the guest house, where Morag Luton's nephew had been expected to spend the weekend. He then took them back to the office, where Dr Cassidy phoned Mrs Horne to ask if Chief Inspector Tansey and Sergeant

Abbot might call on her.

"We've warned the four people who were closest to Mrs Luton that you'd be wanting to speak to them, Chief Inspector, and they may have been surprised — only the family knew that her death was not natural — but they accepted. I thought it best if you saw them in their apartments, in a more relaxed atmosphere, perhaps."

"And probably less likely to upset the even tenor of Evenlode?"

"Quite!" Hugh grinned ruefully. "Not that it's been very even lately. If this kind of thing goes on I suspect we'll be out of business soon."

★ ★ ★

"My dear Dick, how very pleasant to see you, though I wish the reason for your visit was a happier one." Anne Horne kissed the Chief Inspector on both cheeks, and offered her hand to Sergeant Abbot. "Now come and sit down and tell me exactly why you're here. Dr Cassidy said you wanted to question some of poor Morag's friends, but why? It must be important for someone as high-powered as you to be sent, Dick, but surely there's nothing suspicious about her death, is there?"

"It's not a question of suspicion, Aunt Anne. The post-mortem made it quite clear that it was not a natural death," Tansey said gently. "We are treating the matter as a murder inquiry."

"Dear God!" Anne shook her head in bewilderment, so that the loose flesh around her jowls trembled, and she looked her age. "That's dreadful, dreadful! Poor little Morag! At least it didn't happen before she had a chance to enjoy seeing her nephew." She stopped abruptly, and her old eyes stared at Tansey in horror. "You're not saying . . . You don't mean . . . "

"At the moment we have no idea who did it, but of course we want to speak to Professor Luton. Unfortunately he's gone to London, and we don't have an address for him, but we hope to trace him through the London School of Economics. Incidentally, what was your impression of him?"

"My impression of him?" There was

a pause as Anne mustered her thoughts. "He seemed a nice young man. He behaved very well. He was attentive to Morag, and pleasant to all of us. Perhaps he was a little too — too eager to please, but it can't have been easy for him to cope with a bunch of old people, most of whom could have been his grand-parents."

"Everyone liked him?"

"Yes, I'm sure they did, though of course we scarcely knew him. Kenneth Barnard didn't think he was very intelligent, even if he was a professor, but Kenneth has rather high standards. And Dorothy Webb was peeved that he referred to the Inuit as Eskimos, but apart from that — "

"I didn't realize you were such an intellectual lot." Tansey laughed.

"Kenneth is." Anne shared Tansey's amusement. "He speaks several languages, but Dorothy is just — just stupidly pernickety, though I suppose I shouldn't say that. She's forever worrying about something. Incidentally, Dick, I didn't see Morag on Friday morning, but I did see Angus Luton leaving Evenlode, and he was in a terrific hurry. He fairly hurtled down the drive."

"Really." Tansey didn't comment that this contradicted what Sarah Field had told him. "What sort of car was he driving?"

"A Ford Escort. Bright red. I imagine it was hired, unless someone had lent it to him. But I expect Dr Cassidy will know. He keeps a list of the makes and licence numbers of regular guests' cars so that they can be brought round to the front door if anyone asks, like in a hotel. The same applies to the residents. I told you we live very comfortably here. Or we used to," she ended sadly. "I wonder if it will ever be the same again."

★ ★ ★

Waiting outside during the interview, Hugh Cassidy stood and stared out of the corridor window at the curve of the tree-lined drive, the lawn bright-bordered with flowers, the blue sky with its strands of scurrying white cloud. It was a beautiful summer's day, but his thoughts were sombre. He couldn't believe that this time next year the family would still be at Evenlode. What had once been an attainable dream had become a nightmare.

He turned as the door of Anne Horne's apartment opened, and the two detectives came out into the corridor. He hastened to intercept them. "Lady Sarson's waiting for you and Mr Kenneth Barnard is with her. I hope you don't object."

"Not at all," said Tansey.

In the event, however, they found the couple somewhat overwhelming. They hadn't expected Melissa Sarson to look like a raddled film star made up for a major role, and Kenneth Barnard gave them no time to get used to the apartment, the walls of which were literally covered with paintings and drawings.

"Chief Inspector," Barnard said at once in his deep, fruity voice, hardly sparing time for introductions, "someone of your rank wouldn't be here inquiring into Mrs Luton's death if there were no suspicious circumstances surrounding it. So do we take it that poor little Morag Luton was murdered? Because, if that's the truth, there would seem to be only one explanation."

"That's very interesting, sir," Tansey replied neutrally.

Lady Sarson laughed, and then reproached herself. "I was going to say that Mr Barnard had done your work for you, Chief Inspector, but it's a tragic matter. Everyone was fond of Morag Luton. She was a nice woman. Was she really — murdered?"

"We're treating the case as one of murder, yes, Lady Sarson." Tansey turned towards Barnard. "And what is your theory, sir?"

"Well, one asks oneself who would gain by Morag's death. Not any of the residents, and certainly none of the Cassidy clan. That leaves only Angus Luton, Morag's only surviving relative."

"And her heir?" Tansey was not impressed. He had heard this suggestion before.

"Probably, but we don't know for sure. It's not the sort of subject we discuss, Chief Inspector."

Feeling himself reproved, Tansey said coldly, "No subject is taboo during a police inquiry into an alleged murder, sir!" But, as Sergeant Abbot gave one of his warning coughs, he added more gently, "What we need is evidence."

"Of course. And I've got some. First, you might like to know that the man was a phoney."

"What?" Now Tansey really was surprised.

"Chief Inspector, I've lived in the United States and I've visited Canada often. I know something about the university systems there, and I assure you that Angus Luton was no professor. Oh, you can't blame him. He'd written all these letters over the years to his auntie, as he called her, making himself out to be important and saying how well he was doing. Why not? In his place a lot of people would do the same."

"So what do you think his place is, sir?"

"I would surmise that he's a junior teacher in a Canadian High School — the equivalent of an English comprehensive — no more than that. Nothing so grand as a university professor. He didn't even understand the term 'tenure'. He seemed to think that anyone who gets tenure automatically becomes a professor, which is not so."

"Besides," said Lady Sarson, "he wasn't very well educated. He talked about Christ Church *College*, if you please — which no one who was hoping to teach or do research there could possibly call the place."

"I see." Tansey was beginning to feel sorry for Angus Luton. "I gather neither of you liked him."

"He wasn't nearly — " Lady Sarson gave a vague wave with a much-beringed hand as she sought for an appropriate word — "nearly *good enough* for Morag, but luckily she didn't realize it. After all, she and her husband had had no children of their own, and he was her husband's only blood relation. Why shouldn't she be prepared to accept him at face value?"

★ ★ ★

Hugh Cassidy was again waiting at the end of the corridor when Tansey, after expressing many thanks for the help Lady Sarson and Mr Barnard had provided, emerged from the apartment with Abbot.

"Phew!" said Abbot as they walked towards Cassidy. "What did her ladyship mean by 'not good enough for Morag'? Not classy enough, I suppose."

Tansey grinned. "Presumably."

"And what's this tenure business, sir?"

"Security. You can't be sacked from your university job, unless you commit some awful crime."

"Such as murder," Abbot said softly as they came up to Hugh Cassidy.

Cassidy said he would introduce them to Norman Poynter, and then, if they didn't mind, he wouldn't wait; he had work to do. When they had finished with Mr Poynter perhaps they would find their own way to the reception desk, where Sarah would be ready to arrange anything that they wished.

Tansey agreed that would be fine, and asked if Dr Cassidy could let them have any known particulars about the car that Professor Luton had been driving. Cassidy said he'd make a note of the details for them, and added as he rang Norman Poynter's bell, his tired face breaking into a grin, "But I can tell you one thing right now. He'd been giving a ride to a lady the first Saturday he came here. She'd dropped her handkerchief. I noticed it when I was parking the car for him."

Before either Tansey or Abbot could comment, Norman Poynter opened the door and ushered them into his apartment. If Lady Sarson's sitting-room had seemed cluttered, Poynter's was the reverse. It was sparsely furnished with modern pieces, and there was only one very large painting which Tansey thought might be a David Hockney.

"This is a bad business," said Poynter, shaking his fringe of white hair. "Poor Morag! I'm going to miss her. We're all going to miss her. We've been having a bad time at Evenlode recently, as I expect you've heard, and this is the last straw. It's very dispiriting for everyone, and especially for the poor Cassidys. Chief Inspector, I take it there's something suspicious about Mrs Luton's death, or otherwise you wouldn't be here — "

"We're treating the inquiry into Mrs Luton's death as a murder inquiry, certainly, Mr Poynter."

"I assumed that was it. But I find the fact hard to accept, I must admit. Morag Luton is the last person I would think anyone would want to murder."

"Did you see her on Friday morning, Mr Poynter?"

"No, I didn't. I went for my usual early morning swim, had breakfast in the dining-room and then came back here to write letters. We were expecting her to come down to the drawing-room with her nephew for a drink before lunch — we gathered he was arriving during the morning — but I suppose she was dead by then. It's not a happy thought."

"You went to the little party Mrs Luton gave for her nephew, Professor Luton?"

"I did." Blue eyes, suddenly keen, looked directly at Tansey. "And you'd like to know what I thought of him?" Poynter didn't wait for an answer. "I won't ask why. Chief Inspector, in my time I've employed a great many people, and I've learnt to assess character from the appearance and bearing of an individual. Mind you, I haven't always judged accurately. Nevertheless, Angus

Luton didn't impress me. He certainly made an effort to be pleasant to his aunt, and interested in her ancient friends, but it seemed to me a rather obvious effort and I have to admit it crossed my mind that the reason he was paying Morag so much attention was to get something — probably money — out of her. Not a charitable thought, I agree, and I haven't the slightest evidence to support it. But there you are. That was my impression of the professor. Take it for what it's worth."

"I'll do just that, Mr Poynter," said Tansey. "I found it very interesting. Thank you."

★ ★ ★

When the two police officers reached the hall they found that Sarah had the information about Angus Luton's car ready for them, and Tansey asked her to remind Dr Cassidy that a scene of crime team from Headquarters would be arriving later that afternoon to give Mrs Luton's apartment a thorough search. To the disappointment of Abbot, who had hoped to stay until tea-time, he then said they were leaving. They would be back, he agreed, 'in due course'.

The return drive to Kidlington took place in comparative silence. The Chief Inspector appeared deep in thought and Abbot knew better than to interrupt him. When they reached Headquarters, Tansey got out of the car and said, "Meet me in my office, Sergeant. I'm going to phone Ottawa to check up on this Angus Luton. They're five or six hours behind us, so this should be a good time."

Which indeed it proved to be. Tansey got through to Carleton University with no difficulty and asked for Inquiries. He said that he was speaking from England. He needed to get in touch with a Professor Angus Luton in order to consult him on an important matter.

"I'm afraid you're out of luck, sir," came the reply.

"Why?" For a moment Tansey wondered if Kenneth Barnard could be right, but he was immediately disabused of this idea.

"Professor Luton isn't here right now,

sir, and I don't have an address for him. He's on vacation, touring around somewhere. But he's due back early in September if you'd like to leave a message for him to call you."

"No. I hope to catch up with him before then, but thanks," Tansey said and, when Abbot came into the office, he added, "At least that's one supposition disproved, Sergeant. Angus Luton *is* a professor at Carleton University, and not a lowly teacher or anyone else masquerading as a clever academic."

Nevertheless, no one, either at Christ Church or at LSE, appeared to have heard of Angus Luton.

12

THE following day Chief Inspector Tansey drove himself into Oxford to the offices of Messrs Arbuthnot, Crewe & Crewe, Solicitors, where he had an appointment with Mr James Crewe, who had looked after the Lutons' affairs for many years. Having given his name and proffered his warrant card to an attractive young receptionist he was at once shown into a large, modern office, which smelt, not of dusty files, but of furniture polish and air freshener.

Mr James Crewe, in his dark grey suit, white shirt and black tie, fitted somewhat uneasily into this background; the dusty file image would have better suited him. He was, Tansey guessed, in his sixties, a thin, gaunt-looking man, hollow-cheeked and sharp-featured. Half glasses slid down his nose as he stood and offered Tansey a cold bony hand across the desk.

"Good morning, Chief Inspector," he

said in a surprisingly high voice. "Please sit down and tell me how I can be of service." He indicated a chair.

Tansey sat. "As I said when I telephoned, sir, it concerns the estate of the late Mrs Morag Luton. I gather from Dr Cassidy of Evenlode House that you hold her will and would know about the details of her estate."

"Yes, that is so, Chief Inspector, but I fail to understand why that should interest the police."

"Unfortunately it does, sir. I have to inform you that Mrs Luton did not die a natural death, and the police are treating the investigation as a murder inquiry."

James Crewe failed to respond at once. He formed a pyramid with his hands and appeared to study it. Then he said, "I cannot conceive of anyone wanting to kill Morag Luton. Who would gain from her death?"

"Someone, surely, Mr Crewe — an heir — or am I wrong in supposing she was a rich woman?"

"You are both right — and wrong, Chief Inspector. While she lived, Mrs Luton was comfortably off, but her own personal estate is comparatively negligible. Perhaps I should explain."

"I should be grateful," Tansey said, and listened attentively as James Crewe gave a clear and succinct account of the situation.

Philip Luton had been a seriously rich man, but he had had firm ideas concerning money, one of which was that women had no idea how to deal with it. This didn't bother his wife, who was perfectly happy not to have to worry about business. When Mr Luton died he left everything, apart from a few small bequests, to Mrs Luton in trust for her lifetime, an arrangement which she fully understood and with which she agreed.

James Crewe paused. "Any questions so far, Chief Inspector?"

"Yes," said Tansey. "Several, Mr Crewe. I assume the trustees were compelled to make an adequate allowance to Mrs Luton, and had discretionary power to expend capital if an emergency made it necessary or circumstances made it desirable. Otherwise, I don't see how the capital needed to buy the Evenlode House lease became available."

"That is a good question, Chief Inspector, and you are correct in your surmises."

"Then next, Mr Crewe, could this trust be broken?"

Here Mr Crewe gave a large toothy smile. "Chief Inspector, Arbuthnot, Crewe & Crewe is an old firm with an enviable reputation. We would pride ourselves on leaving no loophole in any legal document. However, the trustees were reasonable, and Mrs Luton never showed any desire to break the trust, to which, as I said, she had originally given her full consent."

"I see," said Tansey thoughtfully. "That's all very clear. Now, how big were those small bequests you mentioned? Who received them? And who now owns the lease of Mrs Luton's apartment at Evenlode, which was obviously bought under the trustees' discretion?"

"Again, very sensible questions," said Mr Crewe as if to a promising pupil. "The bequests were to people like the chauffeur and the household staff. In all, they amounted to no more than a few thousand pounds, and were paid immediately after Mr Luton's will was probated. That took place a couple of years ago, so the bequests cannot concern you."

"And the apartment?" Tansey prompted as Mr Crewe paused.

"That is more complex," said Crewe. "However, I will try to explain. Although it was bought in Mrs Luton's name, the unexpired portion of the lease reverts to the trust."

"Which Dr Cassidy has to buy back?"

"You know that?" The solicitor was impressed.

"Yes." Tansey didn't explain how he had come by this information; his relationship with Anne Horne was no business of Crewe's. "What happens to the trust after that?"

"In due course, all the assets will be divided between half a dozen charities and the trust will be dissolved. The Lutons had no children, as I expect you are aware."

"And Mrs Luton's personal estate, which you described as comparatively negligible, Mr Crewe — what happens to that?"

"In accordance with Mrs Luton's own will it will also revert, and form part of the trust."

"I see," said Tansey again, and slowly.

"Which means, as I implied before, and I'm sure you appreciate, Chief Inspector, that no one individual would gain from Mrs Luton's death, and therefore might have reason to kill her."

"As long as they knew the situation," murmured Tansey. Then more loudly, he remarked tentatively, "So Professor Angus Luton inherits nothing whatsoever?"

"Ah! I was waiting for that question." Crewe was pleased with himself. "Nothing is left to Professor Luton, and, what is more, Professor Luton is fully aware of this fact. Several years before he died, Mr Philip Luton, in order to avoid tax, and because his nephew was expecting to get married, made over to him a million dollars, more than half a million pounds at the then rate of exchange, in lieu of an inheritance. The marriage didn't take place. The girl cried off. But of course the gift stood."

"Generous," said Tansey.

"Yes, indeed," Crewe agreed, as his

secretary knocked on the door and came into the office to say that he was wanted on the telephone. He rose and once again offered Tansey his hand. "You must excuse me now, Chief Inspector, but I imagine I shall see you at the inquest this afternoon. In any case, you'll keep in touch, won't you? What you've told me complicates matters sadly, but I hope all the problems will soon be resolved."

★ ★ ★

As Tansey, escaping from this legal verbiage, was about to edge his car out of its parking slot, its phone rang. It was Sergeant Abbot with a message from Dr Cassidy of Evenlode. Cassidy thought the Chief Inspector might like to know that a Mr Alan Appleyard, the manager of a branch of Barclays Bank in Oxford, had been shocked to read of Mrs Luton's death in *The Times* that morning, and had called to ask for details. He had been very insistent, and Dr Cassidy had referred him to the Chief Inspector.

"When was this, Abbot?" asked Tansey.

"Dr Cassidy's call? Fifteen minutes ago, sir. I tried you at once, but there was no answer."

"I was with Mr Crewe. It must have been he who put the notice in *The Times*, and probably in the *Telegraph* too, but he never mentioned doing so. Get a copy, Abbot."

"I've already done that, sir. It merely reads, '*Luton, Morag Elspeth, beloved wife of the late Philip Edward Luton, suddenly at Evenlode House, Oxon. on Friday*' — it gives the date, and adds — '*Funeral details later.*'"

"Not very informative. Thanks, Abbot. I think I'll pay a call on this Mr Appleyard before I come back to HQ."

Leaving the car, Tansey walked to the bank branch. It was a fine day, hot and sunny, but with a hint of thunder in the air. Oxford, out of term, was seething with foreign tourists, delegates to conferences, summer school students and long-suffering residents. Tansey had to elbow his way along the pavement past gaping groups being lectured on the architectural merits and historic importance of various buildings. He was glad to reach his objective.

At least he was not kept waiting. He was at once shown into Mr Appleyard's office. Alan Appleyard, a small round man with receding hair, was clearly upset.

"This is most distressing, Chief Inspector," he said as soon as Tansey was seated. "Most distressing! Mrs Luton was not only a valued client, but almost a — a personal friend. I've known her — and her husband till he died — for several years and I'm truly grieved. *The Times* said 'suddenly', but what does that mean? Did she have an accident? Is that why the police are involved? Dr Cassidy was most reticent."

"No, Mrs Luton's death was not due to an accident, Mr Appleyard," Tansey said slowly. "I regret to tell you that it was not a natural death and the case is being treated as one of murder."

"Murder! How? Why? Who on earth? Dear God!" Appleyard stroked his chin fiercely in a nervous mannerism. "Friday, it said in the paper, but I was speaking to her the day before and she was so bright and happy, so pleased to have her nephew in England." He shook his head in disbelief. "Was it a burglar? A mugger?"

"We don't know who it was yet, but it must have been a quick and comparatively peaceful death."

"I suppose that's something to be grateful for."

"It is indeed, sir, I assure you. You say you were speaking to her on Thursday. What was that about?"

"Nothing important. Her nephew, Professor Angus Luton wanted to open an account with us. Mrs Luton said she'd written him an introductory note, but she'd decided to phone and confirm it. Of course I said we'd be happy to accommodate him."

"And were you?"

"Why, yes. He came in to see me shortly after Mrs Luton's phone call, bearing Mrs Luton's letter — a most attractive young man. He explained that he would be bringing money over from Canada, but meanwhile he'd like to open an account with a small cheque his aunt had given him. He filled in the form, and asked for a temporary cheque-book, which we gave him."

"A *small* cheque?"

"Chief Inspector, I can't discuss my clients' accounts. In my distress at learning of Mrs Luton's death I've already been a little indiscreet, but — "

"Mr Appleyard, this is an official inquiry into a supposed murder!" Tansey bit off each word, startling the bank manager. "Do you want us to be compelled to get a court order?"

"No! Yes! No! I — I understand."

"Then for how much was this *small* cheque?"

"A thousand pounds, which to Mrs Luton really *was* small, Chief Inspector." Suddenly Appleyard seemed distrait. "You're not suggesting for a moment that there was something wrong with the cheque, are you?"

"No, I'm sure it was fine. Anyway, Mrs Luton signed it before her death, and Professor Luton has paid it in."

"Yes, but — " Appleyard looked uncomfortable. "He paid it in on Thursday, and drew it out on Friday morning."

"What? All of it?"

"Nine hundred and fifty pounds."

"But didn't anyone question the withdrawal?"

"The cashier was inexperienced. She merely checked there was enough money in the account, and paid out. Don't forget the original cheque had been drawn on this branch, so there was no question of waiting for clearance."

"Didn't Luton offer an explanation?"

"Yes. I gather he said he'd just found a flat and needed to put down a deposit on it. The rest of his money was in Canada, but he needed this Sterling immediately. You can't blame the girl. It sounds a reasonable explanation, doesn't it?"

"And probably it was quite genuine, Mr Appleyard," said Tansey.

"Let's hope you're right, Chief Inspector. Yes, on second thoughts, I'm sure you must be. You had me worried for a moment, but of course there's no question that Mrs Luton's cheque was good."

Nevertheless, on his way back to his car, Tansey was vaguely perturbed. He realized that a thousand pounds to Angus Luton wouldn't be the same as a thousand pounds to himself or Abbot, but there was an odd inconsistency about the Professor's behaviour. He was coming to Evenlode for the weekend, but changed his mind before he got there, since he hadn't taken his bag into the house. He didn't make much of an effort to find his aunt, nor did he bother to write her a note. He chatted with Sarah and then, according to Anne Horne, drove off down the drive at a furious pace. Above all, why, if he had decided — and it seemed an odd decision in his circumstances — that he couldn't afford to take up a post at Oxford University had he, only hours later, decided to put down a deposit on a flat in that city? It made no sense. But little that Angus Luton had done since coming to England made sense.

★ ★ ★

In the afternoon Chief Inspector Tansey went to the Coroner's Court. The proceedings were very brief. After evidence of identification, Tansey asked formally for an adjournment to give time for further inquiries into the death in suspicious circumstances of Morag Elspeth Luton. The coroner, who had been briefed, acceded without further ado, and the inquest was adjourned *sine die*. The deceased's body was released for burial.

"Thank goodness we can go ahead with the funeral arrangements," said James Crewe, coming up to Tansey. "Mrs Luton left quite strict instructions for which I am responsible."

"May I ask what the instructions were?" inquired Tansey, from politeness rather than interest.

"Certainly." Crewe looked positively happy at the thought of organizing a funeral. "Mrs Luton was not a religious woman in the sense of being a regular churchgoer, and she wanted to be cremated privately and her ashes laid to rest beside her husband's in a memorial rose garden near Edinburgh. I will of course personally see to it that her wishes are carried out, and indeed, in the present distressing circumstances, they are most suitable."

"Most suitable," Tansey agreed, thankful there was to be no local involvement.

"Incidentally, Chief Inspector, I'm not sure I made myself clear this morning. Although Professor Luton is not a beneficiary of Mrs Luton's will, I am still eager to get in touch with him and to inform him of his aunt's unfortunate demise. So if you hear from him . . ."

"I'll let you know, Mr Crewe. We too are trying to trace him."

"Thank you. Thank you, Chief Inspector."

Turning away from Crewe, Tansey almost knocked into a young man who gave him a wide and sardonic smile. "Hello, Chief Inspector," he said. "Let me introduce myself. I'm Michael Balham of the *Colombury Courier* and, needless to say, very interested in the goings-on at Evenlode House."

"So I gather, Mr Balham," said Tansey curtly, "and you seem extremely well informed on the subject."

"Coming from you that's quite a compliment, Chief Inspector."

There was no squashing the bumptious guy, Tansey thought, and with a dismissive nod made to pass him, but Balham blocked his path.

"Are you making any headway with Mrs Luton's murder, Chief Inspector?"

"No comment, Mr Balham."

"Oh come, you mustn't be uncooperative with the Press."

"You heard what the rest of your colleagues heard. The inquest has been adjourned to enable the police to continue with their inquiries. If you'll get out of my way, I can do just that."

But Balham was impervious to remarks of that kind. "What about a different angle, then?" he said. "What is your personal opinion of Evenlode House, Chief Inspector?"

"I have none, Mr Balham."

"That I find difficult to believe, considering you have an old friend of your family in residence there. Mrs Horne, isn't it, a kind of adopted aunt?"

"No comment, Mr Balham. Now, please let me pass."

"OK, Chief Inspector, but if I had an elderly relative I was fond of, I wouldn't let her live at Evenlode House under Dr Cassidy's tender care, I assure you. The good doctor may know a bit more than he did when he had that trouble as a houseman, but I wouldn't bet on it."

Balham's grin had become a knowing leer. Obviously he felt that he had scored a point. With a careless wave he turned and left Tansey standing. Tansey controlled his temper. Simon Cassidy had been right, he thought, when he described Michael Balham as a nasty piece of work. The only thing to do was to ignore him, but . . .

Could there be any truth in the scurrilous remark that Balham had made about Hugh Cassidy and, if so, did it have any relevance?

★ ★ ★

When Tansey returned to Headquarters he was kept busy for some time with paperwork and the telephone, tidying up a previous case and giving a pep talk to a young woman police constable who had been assaulted while helping to arrest a drunk and was having doubts about her career. He also had to study the reports of the various officers at work on other aspects of the Luton case. It was nearer seven than six before he was through, and he wanted to get home to his wife, his baby son and his supper; he wasn't sure in what order of priority he'd have put them. He was tired.

Nevertheless, he went along to the library and took down the *Medical Directory*. There were several Cassidys, but he had no trouble in finding the one he wanted. Hugh Cassidy had trained in Oxford and London, and the usual information was provided. It was not a great help, and the Chief Inspector was faced with the alternative of questioning Hugh Cassidy personally, or seeking out someone who would have been at the same hospital twenty-five years ago, and would have knowledge of the so-called 'trouble' to which Balham had referred. He decided to begin with Cassidy.

Michael Balham had in his malice started a hare which could not be ignored, at least not by such a conscientious police officer as Detective Chief Inspector Dick Tansey.

13

THURSDAY had not begun well at Evenlode House. Everyone was tense, sleeping badly and therefore inclined to be short tempered. Inevitably accidents occurred. Earlier that morning Lucinda had burned her hand rather badly, and Jill, cleaning the apartment of one of the residents, had broken a porcelain ornament, for which — to Patrick's annoyance — the owner had unexpectedly demanded she should pay. Hugh was glad to get away from them all, if only for a short time. The strain of appearing cheerful and confident, when in fact he felt the exact opposite, was telling on him.

He strode through the grounds which, apart from a gardener and his boy, appeared deserted, and he thought of what Michael Balham had written days ago in the *Courier* — how so much land could be better employed than catering for the pleasure of a few. And yet if one considered really large estates, this was unfair. Why didn't Balham attack Ashley Ormonde, for example? Ormonde owned many more acres, and there were only himself, his wife and a widowed daughter to enjoy them.

Hugh Cassidy knew the answer, or thought he did. The *Courier* would never attack Ormonde as long as his buddy, John Rayner, was on the board. But that didn't explain Balham's obvious and vicious vindictiveness against Evenlode. There had been another slashing attack in that morning's paper, suggesting that no resident was safe in his or her bed after Mrs Luton's death, and blaming Dr Cassidy for his failure to recognize at once that her death had not been natural. There had been no mention of Dr Band.

Hugh reached the corner of the property where the dry-stone wall had been knocked down, supposedly by a lorry that hadn't stopped. Two men were busy rebuilding it, but it was slow work.

"Good morning," said Hugh. "How's it going?"

"'Morning, Dr Cassidy. It's going all right, but it's not something you can hurry, like," said one workman in his soft Oxfordshire burr. "It'll take a lot more effort to set it up again than what it took to knock it down."

"It took a real lambasting," the other one said. "The bugger what did it must have been drunk, or he did it on purpose. I don't see how he managed to drive off afterwards. I'd have thought he wouldn't have been able to restart her after the battering she must have taken."

"The lorry, you mean?" said Hugh. "Actually we aren't sure what kind of vehicle did it. Someone did see a lorry going down the lane here, but there's no proof it was the culprit."

"And they haven't caught the bugger, have they? Not surprising. That Sergeant Donaldson wouldn't have the first idea where to start looking." The two nodded in unison; Donaldson was not popular in the district.

"Well, you're doing a fine job," Hugh said, wondering if the stonemason's conjecture could be right, and the wall had been damaged deliberately;

this possibility hadn't occurred to anyone before.

He went off to look at the elm tree that Ashley Ormonde claimed was causing him so much anxiety, but it appeared as firmly rooted as ever. It might come down in a gale, but not before. Hugh sat on the grass and propped his back against the trunk. He shut his eyes. He thought how peaceful it was. But soon his conscience pricked him and he returned, though slowly, to the house.

He stopped in the hall to speak to Sarah before going into the office. "Any excitements?" he asked.

"Mrs Grey phoned. The Greys are bringing Miss Webb back this evening around seven forty-five on their way to dinner. Miss Webb hasn't been well and — according to Mrs Grey — should go straight to bed with a light supper. She added that it was against her wishes that Miss Webb was returning, as personally she didn't consider Evenlode a particularly safe place at the moment. However, Miss Webb had insisted."

"Damn that bloody Grey woman!" Hugh exploded. "Anything else?"

"No, nothing of importance."

A tightness in Sarah's voice alerted Hugh and he looked at her more closely. He saw that her eyes were red, their lids swollen, and he remembered now that she hadn't appeared at breakfast, at least not during the brief time that he had been in the kitchen.

"Sarah, my dear, what's wrong? You've been crying."

"No, I haven't. I'm fine," she lied. "Nothing's wrong."

Hugh didn't believe her. He smiled at her, yearning to comfort her and feeling responsible. "Sarah, I know we're in a mess at the moment, but Evenlode's not going under, not if I can help it. And if the worst comes to the worst, we'll survive — the family will survive, and you're part of it."

"Yes, of course. And thank you," she said.

Luckily the telephone purred at this point and Sarah was able to turn away. Another minute of Hugh's obvious concern and affection for her and she would have burst into tears. She was sincerely grateful to the Cassidys and would have done anything for them — almost anything. But she would *not* stay at Evenlode or anywhere else with them if Simon married Val Rowan.

Waking during the previous night with a headache, Sarah had gone along to Val's room in the hope of borrowing an aspirin. As she reached the door she heard smothered laughter, voices — Simon's voice — and she had crept back to her own bed to weep into the pillow until morning.

Now, by the time she had dealt with the phone call — a resident wishing to bring an unexpected guest to dinner — Hugh had gone, and Val had come into the hall. Sarah waved to her.

"Yes. What is it?" Val approached the reception desk.

"Miss Webb's returning tonight about seven forty-five," said Sarah, thinking that Val looked pretty but not happy — in spite of Simon. "Could you check her apartment, air the rooms and make sure the place is nice for her? Put some flowers in it to welcome her. She'll be going straight to bed."

"OK," said Val indifferently, but she went off on her errand at once without demur.

* * *

Tansey was delayed at Headquarters by a chance meeting with the Chief Constable and then a succession of interruptions, but as soon as he and Abbot reached Evenlode he asked to speak to Dr and Mrs Cassidy, as soon as they could spare the time. He had decided on an indirect approach.

They arrived in the small sitting-room, now the interview room. Tansey could sense their underlying tension, and the depression beneath their friendly, relaxed greetings, and he felt sorry for them. But he had a job to do.

"I want you to tell me about the various incidents that have upset the even tenor of Evenlode of late. There may be — though almost certainly there is not — some connection between them and Mrs Luton's death. Anyway, personally I've learnt to suspect coincidences, and you do seem to have had a spate of disasters recently. Just when did they start?"

"With the thefts," Hugh said at once, and explained in detail.

Then between them they went on to recount the other incidents — the food poisoning, the damage to the stone wall, the vandalism of the pool area, and now a police inquiry. Tansey listened carefully and asked some pertinent questions.

"And everything has received and is still receiving the full glare of publicity," Lucinda said.

"So I had observed," said Tansey. "You must have wondered if you had an enemy intent on ruining you."

"We have wondered that, yes," Hugh admitted, "but the idea's absurd. We traced the thief, as I told you, and the food poisoning must have been accidental — though I haven't received the lab reports yet. The stone wall could have been damaged deliberately, though we didn't think of that when it happened, but equally well the damage may not have been deliberate. As for the vandals, they were probably incited by articles in the *Courier*."

"But the idea of killing poor Morag in order to do us down . . . " Lucinda shook her head.

"No, I agree. That would seem a little far-fetched," Tansey replied, but he was not so sure about the other incidents. "You don't believe you have an enemy, then? Someone you sacked once upon a time? Someone who might bear you a grudge?"

"There was the Wilson girl we sacked for stealing, of course, and we have a neighbour called Ashley Ormonde who dislikes us and who's a chum of one of the *Courier*'s directors — a chap named John Rayner, who's also an uncle of Balham's," said Hugh. "But I wouldn't describe any of them as enemies. It's much too strong a word, and they would have nothing to gain by ruining us. No, Chief Inspector, it simply isn't possible to make a logical pattern out of our recent misfortunes."

"What about someone who might bear either of you a grudge from a supposed wrong done many years ago?"

Hugh and Lucinda stared at him, and then at each other. Neither spoke, and

218

Tansey wondered if Michael Balham had lied, or if he had made a mountain out of a molehill and the Cassidys had forgotten the matter.

"Twenty-five years ago," he prompted, "when Dr Cassidy was a junior doctor. There was some trouble at the hospital, I'm told."

"Who told you? Who's resurrected *that* old story?" Lucinda asked sharply.

So Balham hadn't lied, Tansey thought, nor had he exaggerated some trifling happening that the Cassidys had forgotten. It was obvious they well remembered the incident to which Balham had referred, and that it had been and still was important to them. Their first response to his question had been one of shock. Now Lucinda was flushed with indignation, and Hugh had become whey-faced.

"I think you'd better tell me about it," Tansey said.

"There's not much to tell," Hugh answered readily enough. "A woman collapsed at a party and was brought to casualty by her drunken friends. I didn't question her friends closely or examine her with enough care. She died in the night. It wasn't until her husband arrived at the hospital the next morning that I learnt she was a diabetic. Unfortunately he hadn't been at the party."

"Hugh wasn't to blame," Lucinda said vehemently. "He'd been on duty for seventy-three hours, and he was exhausted. Of course, there was a fuss. It shouldn't have happened. The poor woman ought not to have died. But she wasn't wearing any kind of diabetic warning bracelet, and none of her friends mentioned her complaint. It was their fault — or her own fault — as much as Hugh's. No one at the hospital blamed him. The press made a thing of it, of course, but mostly because of the hours housemen worked."

"What was the name of the woman?" Tansey asked.

"Anthea Montague-Stott," said Hugh, "and her husband's name was James." He gave a bitter laugh. "But that's not going to help you, Chief Inspector. Mr Montague-Stott is dead — he was a lot older than his wife, and so is his only brother, and all four parents — and the Montague-Stotts had no children who might have been waiting twenty-five years to exact revenge."

"Dr Cassidy, it has been known for people to wait considerably longer than a quarter of a century before exacting revenge, as you put it, but I agree it doesn't seem very likely in this case. However, I'm sure you appreciate that once the story had been brought to my attention I had to look into it."

"Of course," Hugh agreed.

"But who brought it to your attention, Chief Inspector?" Lucinda demanded.

Tansey hesitated. Then, "Michael Balham," he said, "which possibly means some more unpleasant publicity."

"Damn!" Lucinda swore.

Hugh sighed. "It can't be helped. It's surprising he's taken so long to unearth this item from my murky past. Incidentally, Chief Inspector, while I remember — Miss Dorothy Webb is returning to Evenlode this evening. She was fairly friendly with Mrs Luton and she was at the party Mrs Luton gave for her nephew. I doubt if she can tell you anything of interest, but if you'd like to speak to her I could make sure she'll be available tomorrow."

"Thank you. Tomorrow morning will be fine. We'll leave you in peace till then."

* * *

When they were alone in the car Sergeant Abbot, who hadn't spoken a word throughout the interview with the Cassidys, said, "Where to now, sir? It's a little early for lunch."

"Which you were hoping to get at Evenlode?" Tansey grinned. "Hard luck, Abbot. We'll sample the Windrush Arms today, but first we're going to pay a visit to the Wilsons — the girl who was sacked for stealing and her mother. Mrs Cassidy said they came from the village, so we can probably get their address from the general store."

"Right, sir."

The village of Evenlode was only minutes away by car and, as Tansey had suggested, there was no difficulty in finding out where the Wilsons lived. It was a small cottage and, if it didn't have roses growing around the door, it was certainly picturesque, its Oxfordshire stone having mellowed to the colour of a honeycomb.

Mrs Wilson was not welcoming. After a long pause on the doorstep while they identified themselves, "I suppose you'd better come in," she said reluctantly.

Inside, the cottage was not unattractive, though Tansey suspected that its essential utilities were primitive. Mrs Wilson showed them into the front room, and gestured to them to sit down.

"I don't understand what you want," she said. "Dr Cassidy promised there'd be no comeback from what Zena's supposed to have done."

"Mrs Wilson, this isn't any comeback, as you call it. Dr Cassidy doesn't even know we're here. We just want you to tell us about the thefts at Evenlode House."

"I'll tell you something, Inspector!"

"Chief Inspector!" Abbot corrected her.

Doreen Wilson ignored him. "As I was saying, if I'd known then what I know now, I wouldn't have gone so tamely. But Zena had been in trouble before — once — and there was all the evidence in front of my eyes. Mind you, I don't blame Dr Cassidy, or that nice Patrick. I'd have done the same in their place."

"Mrs Wilson, please!" Tansey interrupted. "Start at the beginning."

Mrs Wilson's account differed very little from the Cassidys', though inevitably there was a shift in emphasis as she described her feelings, her indignation at the accusation, her pleasure when she seemed to be proved right, then her dismay — turning to anger against Zena — when the girl's guilt became apparent.

"Poor Zena!" her mother said. "She denied it, but I didn't believe her — not at the time. How could I? There were all those missing things in her hold-all. But I've changed my mind since." She paused for a moment, then, staring Tansey straight in the eye, added, "It's my opinion now that she was framed, though I've no hope of proving it."

"Framed?" Tansey repeated mildly. He wasn't surprised by Doreen Wilson's final remark; it was quite clear to him that she had been leading up to some conclusion. "What made you decide that, Mrs Wilson?"

"Well, Zena's not a bad girl. She's simple, like, but she's not a liar. The time she pinched some clothes from a store she admitted to it, but this time even when we got home she went on and on swearing she'd never taken anything from Evenlode House. She almost convinced me, and I began to think about the money."

"What money?"

"Sir, there was said to have been about fifty pounds in Mr Poynter's wallet," Abbot prompted. "And we were told Miss Webb lost thirty pounds."

"Ah yes, I remember. Mr Poynter's always losing his possessions and no one thought the wallet had been stolen until it turned up in Zena's bag — empty."

"So what happened to that money — Mr Poynter's and Miss Webb's? That's what I asked myself, Inspector," said Mrs Wilson.

"Chief Inspector," Abbot murmured automatically.

Mrs Wilson turned her boot-button eyes briefly to Abbot. "Chief Inspector, if Zena took that money what did she do with it? I searched her room. No money. No new clothes or bits and pieces. Not that she's had much chance to get to the shops recently to spend any of it. I've been keeping a strict eye on her. So what's she done with that money? There's only one answer. She never had it. Do you follow me?"

"I do indeed, Mrs Wilson. It's very logical reasoning. But why should anyone want to frame your daughter?"

"I've no idea, unless it's just someone being mischievous, but it's not exactly that sort of household, is it, not with all them oldies?" Surprisingly, Doreen Wilson laughed aloud. Then she became serious. "But as I said before there's no proof and no hope of any unless the real thief turns up."

"Have you found a new job?" Tansey asked, conscious that it was not strictly his business.

"Three mornings a week, and Zena's helping out at the farm for her meals and some pocket money. It's a kindness on Mrs Cuddlestone's part really, and I'm grateful. It's bad for Zena to have nothing to do. But of course it's not like Evenlode House," Doreen Wilson ended wistfully.

* * *

Later in the afternoon of that Thursday Chief Inspector Tansey sat across the desk from his Chief Constable, Philip Midvale. They were discussing the death of Morag Luton, and the unusual circumstances surrounding it.

"So this Mrs Wilson convinced you of her daughter's innocence?" said Midvale dubiously.

"That would be putting it too strongly, sir, but everyone agrees that Zena is a simple girl, not too bright in the head, and if she found or stole the money it's extremely unlikely she'd have had the cunning to conceal it from her mother. Why should she have tried? She kept the other stolen articles in her hold-all."

"All right, Chief Inspector. We'll assume she *was* framed. Who framed her, and why?"

"I think that's really one question, sir. I believe the thefts were the first in a series of incidents designed to ruin the Cassidys, or at least their reputation. The second incident, the food poisoning, which was at first considered to be accidental, we now know was deliberate. Cassidy had enough sense to send some samples from one of his patients to the lab, and we've been able to intercept their report. In fact, though Cassidy won't know till tomorrow, the samples contained minute amounts of paradichlorobenzine — it's found in insecticides and deodorants — which was almost certainly in the veal and mushroom casserole. In small quantities the symptoms simulate food poisoning — abdominal pain, nausea, vomiting, diarrhoea. But it was a dangerous game someone was playing; the stuff's poisonous all right. So that incident was for real. The rest of them present no difficulties to my theory. Only Mrs Luton's death doesn't fit, though I can't help feeling there should be a connection."

"But there's nothing to suggest what the connection could be, is there? We can't assume that this would-be destroyer of the Cassidys, killed Morag Luton."

"No, sir, and Angus Luton, who was the most likely suspect to have killed Mrs Luton, has absolutely no motive. Nor, for that matter, has anyone else a motive that we've been able to discover. Still, the Professor does seem to have behaved oddly."

"You haven't traced him yet?"

"No, sir. No one at LSE seems to have heard of him, and he hasn't attempted to make contact with Evenlode, as he told Miss Field he would. I've been in touch with the Met, to see if they can track him down."

"He can't have disappeared into thin air. You must find him, Chief Inspector. He might well be able to answer some of our questions, even though it's obvious he's been in no position to cause the incidents we've been discussing. For that matter, there can't be a great number of people who have been in such a position."

"I appreciate that, sir, but in fact there's really no one who fills the bill, except possibly Patrick Donne or Simon Cassidy, but they've got more to lose than gain if Evenlode goes under. I can't imagine any of the women deliberately driving a vehicle into a stone wall or knowing how to wreck the swimming pool — and what would they gain?"

"You've checked out those who aren't actually real Cassidys — Donne and Field and Rowan. And of course you've noted that these incidents seem to have started with the appearance of Miss Rowan on the scene."

"Yes, on both counts, sir. I've had reports on the three of them, and there's absolutely nothing against them. None of them is related in any way to James or Anthea Montague-Stott, so any idea of revenge for what happened twenty-five years ago is out as far as they're concerned."

"Tell me a bit more about them — Donne and Field and Rowan, I mean."

"Well, Patrick Donne appears to enjoy his marriage and his job. Sarah Field, who is a very capable woman, is, I guess, in love with Simon and hoped to marry him, but the arrival of pretty Valerie Rowan seems to have altered that scenario. I suppose Field might be trying to get her own back on Simon by ruining the Cassidys, but I can't really believe it; it would be more to the point to go for Valerie Rowan, I should think. And Rowan's story stands up, though Inspector Whitelaw who checked it reports that the girlfriend she had expected to stay with in Oxford — a Mrs June Green — was nervous and didn't inspire him with confidence."

"So you think it's just chance these incidents coincided with Rowan's arrival at Evenlode?"

Tansey shrugged. "The first theft — Mr Poynter's wallet — happened *before* she arrived, sir."

"He could have lost it, perhaps down the side of a chair — you tell me he's always losing things — and when she found it she was tempted by the money."

"Yes, sir," said Tansey, who had thought of this possibility himself. "But why the other thefts, and why frame Zena?"

"Why indeed, Chief Inspector? There seem to be more questions than answers at the moment in this case." The Chief

Constable leant back in his armchair, stretching himself warily in an effort to relax his arthritic joints. He indicated that the interview was over. "Anyway, good luck, Tansey, and don't forget that our concern is with Mrs Luton's killer rather than the Cassidys' troubles."

"I won't, sir," said Tansey, who was becoming more and more convinced that the two ingredients of the case had to be connected, though he couldn't have given his reasons.

14

DOROTHY WEBB was deposited at the front door of Evenlode House at seven-forty that evening. The chauffeur had carried her bag but the Greys, on their way to a dinner-party, had not got out of the car because the weather was inclement. The sky was full of thunderheads and the air was sultry; it had started to drizzle. A storm was on its way.

Miss Webb was glad to be back, to be home; in spite of her expectations, she had not enjoyed the few days she had spent with her loving sister. Most of the time she had been in bed, suffering from a chill, and though she had been cared for, it had seemed grudging care. She had been made to feel a nuisance, and had been hesitant to ask for assistance, even when her tea was totally forgotten one afternoon; she hated making unnecessary fusses. But here at Evenlode everyone was so kind they never considered any demand a fuss.

The Evenlode 'family' had been watching for her arrival. The front door had swung open before the chauffeur had regained his seat behind the wheel of the car, and she didn't turn to wave to her sister as she heard the vehicle drive off. Jill was greeting her. Patrick had seized her bag. She gave them both her warmest smile.

"What a shame you've been unwell, Miss Webb," said Jill. "I hope you're feeling better."

"Much better, thank you. It was just a summer cold."

"Not very sensible to be ill on holiday," Patrick chided.

"Not a bit sensible," Dorothy Webb agreed. She never minded Patrick's teasing. "How is everyone here?" and, remembering, hurried on. "I was so sorry to hear about Mrs Luton. She was such a nice woman, and it was kind of her to ask me to that party, though I can't say I cared for her nephew much."

"Yes, Mrs Luton's death is extremely sad," Jill said carefully. "We're all grieved by it."

"I don't understand how anyone would want — I suppose it was a tramp, someone like that." Miss Webb, relaxed, was prepared to chatter.

"No one knows how it happened, Miss Webb," Patrick prevaricated. "The police are making inquiries."

"Here we are!" Jill said with relief as they reached Miss Webb's apartment; she didn't want to be drawn into a lengthy discussion of Morag Luton's death. "I expect your sister was right, and you'd prefer to go straight to bed and have supper brought to you. You must tell me what you'd like to eat."

"That would be wonderful!"

Dorothy Webb had gone ahead of them into the sitting-room. Although she had been away for several days the air smelt fresh, or as fresh as one could expect in this oppressive heat. There were roses in a vase, and she did not need to ask if her houseplants — of which there were many — had been watered. Even her bed, she found, had been turned down. There were no letters, but she hadn't been expecting any.

"Mother's busy with dinner at the

moment," Jill said, "but she'll be along to see you in the morning."

"Thank you. Thank her. It's good to be back."

"Good night, Miss Webb. Sleep well," Patrick called.

"Good night, Patrick, and thank you," she replied.

Five minutes later Jill, having learnt what Miss Webb would like for supper, left her to get to bed. Dorothy Webb was more than contented.

★ ★ ★

"How's Miss Webb?" Lucinda asked at once as Jill came into the kitchen. "Patrick says she's in good form."

"Yes, she is," Jill agreed. "Surprisingly good form, though she doesn't look so great. I think she was probably quite ill at the Greys', but didn't admit it. You know what she's like."

"Yes, but when you take her supper, Jill, make sure she knows that if she feels in the least unwell in the night she must press her emergency button. It doesn't matter what time it is."

"Will do, Mum."

"Did you tell her that the Chief Inspector would want to speak to her tomorrow morning?" Hugh Cassidy asked as he came into the kitchen.

"No, I didn't, Dad. I thought it would only worry her and she might not sleep. Surely breakfast time tomorrow will be soon enough, won't it?"

"Sure, Jill. That was sensible of you."

★ ★ ★

Dorothy Webb woke with a start, her heart pounding. Someone was in her apartment. Her eyesight might be deteriorating, but there was nothing wrong with her hearing and she was positive she had heard a dull thud, what could have been a muffled curse, followed by silence and the whisper of soft steps outside the bedroom door. Her eyes half closed, she listened hard.

But there was a sudden rumble of thunder and a gust of wind stirred the trees, drowning any other sounds there might have been. Dorothy told herself that she had been mistaken. The storm that was brewing must have woken her, and she had either imagined the various noises or they had been the remnants of a nightmare. Nevertheless, she lay rigid, unable to relax, her heart still thudding. Carefully she opened her eyes.

Although the curtains were drawn back so that what air there was might penetrate the room through the two small windows open above the casements, she could see nothing. It was very dark. Then a flash of lightning illuminated the scene, and in its light she saw the door of the bedroom open and a black shape, too substantial to be a shadow, move into the room and towards her bed.

She yearned to scream. She opened her mouth but no sound came. She knew she was going to die, and the thought immediately crossed her mind that this was how Morag Luton had died. But she didn't want to die and, as the cushion descended towards her face, she flung herself sideways and her attacker, caught off balance, fell on top of her. She could feel his weight pressing her down, and accepted that, though she was not as small and frail as Morag had been, she would be no match for him.

Perhaps at this point she would have given up and accepted her fate, in spite of her instinct to reject it, but she was suddenly aware that without realizing it her fingers had sought the emergency button, whose flex Jill had carefully pinned to the sheet, so that it would be within easy reach if she felt she needed it during the night. Its light shone a dull red. She had been pressing it for some moments. Help would be on its way.

Heartened, she renewed her struggle and, raising a bony leg, managed to knee her assailant in the groin. He cried out, but the pain roused him to further effort and, as there was a particularly loud clap of thunder directly overhead, Dorothy Webb felt the cushion press firmly down on her face.

★ ★ ★

The storm had woken the Cassidys and Hugh, slipping on a gown, had gone along the corridor to make sure that the end windows were shut before the rains came. He had just returned to their bedroom when the alarm sounded. A quick glance at the display board on the wall showed where the emergency was.

"Dorothy Webb, Cindy. You'd better follow me," he said.

Seizing his medical bag, Hugh ran. The stairs were quicker than the lift and he ran down them two at a time and tore along the corridor. Slightly breathless, he reached Miss Webb's ground-floor apartment in the west wing. As he inserted his pass key in the lock and entered the small hall, he thought he heard scrabbling noises in the sitting-room but paid them no attention. He went straight through to the bedroom, switching on lights.

Dorothy Webb lay on her back. She was breathing fast, but otherwise appeared unharmed. She managed to give Hugh Cassidy a crooked smile.

"A man — a man was trying to smother me, but I knew you'd come," she gasped. She thrust from her the cushion she had been clutching to her chest. "Take it away. I — I never did like that cushion. I don't want to see it again ever. Ah, Mrs Cassidy," she added as Lucinda came into the room. She repeated what she had told Hugh, adding, "Oh I — I should so love some tea."

"Of course," Lucinda said after a quick glance at Hugh to receive his confirmatory nod. "I'll get it at once."

"While I make sure Miss Webb's all right," Hugh said, opening his bag.

"You — you are both so kind." Suddenly Dorothy Webb burst into tears.

"Shock!" Hugh murmured to Lucinda. "Make the tea — strong and sweet — and check the sitting-room. I think I heard someone getting out that way."

"OK."

Lucinda went first to the kitchenette to put on the kettle, and then into the sitting-room. She saw at once that Hugh had been right. The casement window was wide open, swinging on its hinges as the wind gusted, and the rain was blowing in. A vase of roses had been knocked over, water and flowers spilt on to the carpet. She hesitated before shutting the window or touching anything, but decided to do so carefully, using two fingers only. As she shut the window with some difficulty she heard the bang and growl of thunder, but it was in the distance. The storm was receding.

"We're all locked up and safe," she said a few minutes later as she took the tea into the bedroom.

"Good!" Hugh smiled at her. "Miss Webb's luckily none the worse for her nasty experience, but it must have been shaking, and I've told her you'd spend the rest of the night on the sofa in the sitting-room to keep her company."

There was only the merest question-mark at the end of Hugh's statement; he and Lucinda understood each other very well.

"That's just what I proposed to do — if Miss Webb doesn't mind," Lucinda said.

"How could I mind? I'm only too grateful. I'd be much happier if you were here, Mrs Cassidy."

"That's fine," said Hugh. "Then I'll be off. You'll be all right for a minute while Lucinda gets a duvet, won't you, Miss Webb? It's most unlikely the intruder's hanging about outside, especially in this weather. But I'll certainly go and have a look around."

"Thank you," said Dorothy.

As Lucinda went into the corridor with Hugh, she said, "Hugh, what about the police? Shouldn't we call them at once, and at least leave a message for the Chief Inspector?"

"I've been thinking about that. If I do, they'll come swarming all over the place and disturbing Miss Webb. I've given her a sedative and she should sleep. Tansey can wait till the morning. Anyway, what could he do now? But I will look around outside."

"Be careful," said Lucinda.

"Don't worry, Cindy, I will."

★ ★ ★

Hugh Cassidy telephoned Kidlington early, and by eight o'clock Tansey was on his way to Evenlode House with Abbot and a WPC Morton, a capable and comforting woman who would be able to watch over Miss Webb and ensure her continued safety. Their car was followed by a van containing a team of officers prepared to search the grounds of Evenlode and, it was hoped, Miss Webb's apartment.

The storm had passed, but the rain had been heavy in the night and, as the sun rose, the ground steamed in the heat. It was not the best of days to find clues to the intruder's identity out of doors; if he had left any, they would have been washed away long ago. But it was necessary to go through the motions. The apartment from which he had fled in haste seemed more promising.

Fortunately, Miss Webb, after her tea and a strong sedative, had slept well, secure in the knowledge that Lucinda Cassidy was within call, and she had no intention of being interviewed by police officers while she was in bed. She did not consider it seemly. Moreover, she was secretly rather proud of the way she had behaved — rightly so — and she had no intention of failing in her duty now.

While the police, who had found no joy in the grounds of Evenlode, set to work on Dorothy Webb's apartment, Miss Webb sat opposite Chief Inspector

Tansey in what was at present the interview room, and told her story. He listened without interruption. He had already heard what Hugh and Lucinda Cassidy had had to say, but this was first-hand evidence.

Miss Webb, however, was not a good witness. She jumped from what she had heard and seen to what she thought she might have heard and seen. There was no logical sequence in her discourse, and she seemed to resent simple questions.

"Of course I'm sure it was a man, Chief Inspector. It was a hot, sticky night. I was wearing a thin nightgown and covered only by a sheet. As we struggled he lay right on top of me and I could feel him. I may be a spinster lady, but I assure you he was a man. I would know the difference. I kneed him and he cried out."

There was a strangled sound from WPC Morton, which she quickly turned into a cough. Tansey was thankful that Abbot was not with them. The Sergeant was busy with other officers questioning all the residents — especially those who had apartments near Miss Webb's — in the unlikely event that they might have noticed anything suspicious during the night.

"Er — you can't describe this man, Miss Webb," Tansey said. "For instance, was he shorter or taller that Dr Cassidy?"

"Shorter — I think. As I said, I caught the merest glimpse of him in a lightning flash. He was just a dark figure."

"You never saw his face?"

"No. He had some sort of cover over his head. I felt it. A stocking mask?"

"Could be," Tansey agreed.

"Oh, there's one other thing. His breath smelt of gin. My brother-in-law drinks gin, so I'm quite certain that's what it was."

Tansey nodded, thinking that perhaps the intruder had needed Dutch courage before trying to smother a second old lady, for unless there were two killers on the loose, this attempt had to be connected with Mrs Luton's death. Indeed, the method, the use of a cushion, was identical. But how had the man known there would be a suitable cushion available in Miss Webb's apartment? It was a fair guess, Tansey supposed, but surely the intruder would have wanted to be sure. And, for that matter, how had he known where Miss Webb slept?

"I'm sorry I can't be more helpful, Chief Inspector." Dorothy Webb shook her head, irritated with herself.

"You've done extremely well, Miss Webb," Tansey answered her. "Perhaps you could now turn your mind away from your unpleasant experience to a matter that's probably related. You were a friend of Mrs Luton's, I believe?"

"A friend? I'm not sure I would have claimed her as a friend. In fact I was surprised she invited me to the party she gave for her nephew, though she was always very kind."

"Did you like Professor Luton?"

Dorothy Webb hesitated. "We only exchanged a few words, but I didn't find him particularly agreeable. For one thing, he talked about Eskimos, which, coming from a Canadian professor, I considered insulting to the Inuit. I wonder how he would have liked to be called a Canuck?"

"I wonder," Tansey said. He was

growing a little tired of Miss Webb and, after all, there was no doubt that Angus Luton was a professor at Carleton University, as he claimed to be, whatever he might call the Inuit. "What about the Wednesday he came to dinner here?"

"I saw him across the dining-room and bowed to him. But I don't understand, Chief Inspector. You can't suspect — "

"No, Miss Webb, I don't. Now, tell me what you did on Friday morning, the morning Mrs Luton died."

Dorothy Webb sighed. Her earlier pleasure and excitement at being the centre of interest had ebbed. She was beginning to feel tired. Having to recount the horrors of the previous night to a complete stranger had proved more of a strain than she had expected, and she was still suffering from the after-effects of the severe chill that had reduced her to bed during her visit to the Greys.

"Friday morning, Miss Webb," Tansey repeated, subduing his impatience.

"I went to stay with my sister. She was meant to be coming to fetch me, but . . . "

Nothing would hurry Miss Webb, and

the effort of telling the story revived her. She explained at length how she had packed the night before, but had changed her mind and decided to take a different dress, which had meant that she had to repack in the morning. Then she discovered a seam had come unstitched, but she couldn't thread a needle.

"It was one thing after another," she said, "and it was the final blow when Miss Field told me my sister couldn't fetch me and I'd have to go by bus. If Mrs Horne hadn't been kind enough to drive me to Colombury and — and make sure I was all right, I don't know what I'd have done. Unfortunately, Chief Inspector, these days I'm quite capable of getting on the wrong bus," she admitted.

"Yes," said Tansey meaninglessly, and steeled himself against Dorothy Webb's wistful smile. He had to jog her out of her complacency. "Miss Webb," he said forcefully, "last night someone tried to kill you in the same way that Mrs Luton was killed. The chances are a million to one against him picking you out of the blue. He had a reason. He believes you know something that could lead the police to him. Think! What could it be?"

Dorothy Webb regarded him steadily. "I have thought, Chief Inspector. I'm not a fool. Of course I've asked myself, why me? But I can't think of any answer. I never heard or saw anything out of the ordinary the day poor Morag died. I was much too concerned with my own affairs to worry about other people, and I left Evenlode well before noon. All I can suggest is that he mistook my apartment for someone else's."

"That's possible," Tansey agreed.

But he didn't believe it. Miss Webb's apartment was at the end of the wing and easy to locate. None of her neighbours, according to Dr Cassidy, had been more than acquainted with Morag Luton or had met her nephew.

Why do I keep on coming back to her nephew? Tansey wondered. But to that question also there was no answer. He told himself he must concentrate on essentials. The first thing was to make sure no one had a second chance to kill Miss Dorothy Webb.

15

SERGEANT ABBOT gave an expressive shrug. "Report negative, sir. The intruder got in through the sitting-room window, as we know. He left a fragment of material — as he departed hurriedly, I guess — but almost certainly it's worthless. He wore gloves. No prints. A motorbike tyre mark across a small spillage of oil on the drive near the gates suggests his means of transport — if the mark was made by *his* motorbike, which we can't tell."

"Did anyone hear a motorbike?"

"No, sir. Several of the residents were awake during the night because of the storm, and some even looked out of their windows, but that gave us no help. No one saw anything. On the contrary, the weather was an advantage to our chappie. It explained away whatever noises he might have made."

"Yes, he was lucky," said Tansey ruminatively. "He can't have known

251

there would be a storm the first night Miss Webb was back at Evenlode. The first night," he repeated. "How the hell did he know that, Abbot — that she would be back last night?"

"He might have been watching the place, or — "

"Or someone tipped him off?"

"But who, sir? It seems to me that this case is gathering a fine collection of loose ends."

"You're right. Nevertheless, it was foolish of him to use the same method, tying the two attacks together. The trouble is, Sergeant, that that's the only thing that does tie them together. Miss Webb has been no real help. If she does know something that would give us a strong lead she has no idea what it might be. However, that doesn't mean she's safe. As long as the killer believes she could be a danger to him he might have another go at her, so I've instructed WPC Morton to stick to her like a limpet. And I'd like a twenty-four hour guard on Evenlode."

"Who by? We've not got the men, sir."

"Sergeant Donaldson will have to provide them."

"He can't, sir. He's already short-staffed at the Colombury station. He'll claim that round the clock protection will drain him of resources."

Tansey sighed. "Yes, I suppose you're right, Abbot. OK. We'll make it from ten at night till eight in the morning, but I'd better have a chat with Dr Cassidy. Do you know where he is?"

"He's gone to look at that wretched elm tree of his, see what damage it's done."

"You mean it's blown down? That chap — what's his name? — Ormonde has been proved right after all?"

"I'm not too sure of the facts, sir. I just happened to overhear the gardener telling Dr Cassidy the tree was down on Mr Ormonde's property."

"Poor Cassidy," said Tansey. "All the same, I need to speak to him. Find him, and get him in. He's the man ultimately responsible for Evenlode."

And it was evident when Hugh Cassidy appeared that the responsibility was weighing heavily upon him. He was pale and drawn as he flung himself into the chair opposite Tansey.

"This is the end, Chief Inspector. I really don't think we can take much more. If I believed that this lawyer's offer was a practical proposition I'd be tempted to get out of Evenlode."

Tansey drew a short breath. He yearned to ask, "What lawyer? What offer?" but thought that at the moment this was an irrelevant issue. He told Hugh Cassidy about the precautions he was taking to protect Miss Webb and Evenlode House.

Cassidy was not impressed; in his dealings with Sergeant Donaldson, he had not found him especially cooperative. "Chief Inspector," he said, "are you sure these so-called precautions are necessary? The residents are getting more and more jittery with police all over the place. Already several of them have decided to go away for a few days, and relatives are phoning to ask what's going on here and expressing concern. At least one of them has threatened to try to break the lease her mother has with us."

"Dr Cassidy, I'm sorry, but I've got my

duty to do too, and a third — possibly successful — attempt to kill a resident of Evenlode isn't going to help you."

"No, of course not. I'm sorry. What's important is that everyone should be safe. Ah, dear God! I'm afraid I'm not thinking straight, Chief Inspector." Hugh Cassidy collected his wits and gave a smile that was more like a grimace. "I've been worrying about this bloody elm when — "

"Tell me what's happened to the elm," Tansey interrupted.

Hugh Cassidy glanced at the Chief Inspector curiously; he didn't understand the workings of the police mind. Why should Tansey care about the elm?

"Some time during the night the tree came down across a corner of my property, where my land marches with my neighbour's — that's Ashley Ormonde. It's destroyed some of my drystone wall, and a good deal more of his. The tree will have to be removed and Ormonde will want his pound of flesh. But that's just another blow."

"Was the tree struck by lightning?"

"No, but the wind was gusting up to

fifty or sixty miles per hours."

"So you're not in the least suspicious?"

"Chief Inspector, at the moment I suspect everything and everybody, but I inspected the tree carefully and if it was pulled over by a tractor no one would ever prove it. Anyway, it hardly matters any more."

Tansey gave him a sympathetic glance. "Earlier you mentioned a lawyer's proposition, Dr Cassidy. Were you referring to Mr James Crewe?"

"No, but to an equally reputable firm. They have a consortium of clients who would be prepared to buy Evenlode, but the offer was laughable, even in the distressing circumstances we're in at present. And anyway I don't want to sell, Chief Inspector. It would leave me and my wife, Simon, the Donnes and Sarah in dire straits, and with colossal debts."

"Have you heard from Mr James Crewe?"

"Yes, and he's been very helpful. He expects to arrange for Mrs Luton's furniture and possessions to be removed from her apartment at the beginning of next week, and he's given permission for us to redecorate it."

"And what about the lease?"

"I've got three months from the date Mrs Luton's will is probated to re-sell, or buy back the part that has not expired — which is most of it. I might have begged for more time if an individual had inherited, but as it goes to a trust that's impossible, and my bank's not keen to lend us any more. So in the present circumstances all I can do is hope for a new resident or an unexpected windfall — and the sooner the police can clear up this nasty business, Chief Inspector, the more likely it is that some such miracle might come about."

"I wish I could be encouraging, Dr Cassidy, but unfortunately at the moment the police need a stroke of luck too," Tansey said, and thought that this was indeed the truth.

★ ★ ★

It was after lunch, a lunch that had delighted Sergeant Abbot, before Tansey decided to leave Evenlode House. There was nothing more he could do there.

257

WPC Morton would stay close to Miss Webb, and from ten o'clock in the evening two police officers would patrol the grounds, one of them with a fully-trained Alsatian; there would be a guard at the gates, and residents had been asked to say if they would be out late. Tansey hoped it would be enough.

The car phone buzzed as Abbot reached the end of the drive, turned on to the road and, accelerating, left Evenlode House behind. Tansey reached for the receiver.

"Detective Chief Inspector Tansey," he snapped.

"Inspector Whitelaw here, sir. We've at last traced the source from which Professor Luton hired his Ford Escort. A garage in Cowley — not the kind of place I'd have expected. The proprietor — a man call Albert Bromley — is a rather dubious character, though we've not been able to pin anything on him — yet. Shall I go along or — "

"No. I'll go myself."

Tansey noted the details and passed them on to Abbot. He was intrigued by the information Whitelaw had produced.

Angus Luton, he thought, was always doing the unexpected. The obvious thing for a Canadian arriving at Heathrow to do was to hire a car from one of the big companies — Hertz or Avis, for example — but apparently this was not the Professor's style. He had preferred an obscure garage with a doubtful reputation. Why?

The Chief Inspector had found no answer to that question by the time they had located the garage, which seemed to consist of a forecourt with petrol pumps and a ramshackle building in need of a coat of paint. To one side was a large used car lot. As Abbot drew up a man came out of what was presumably the office. He was short and dark and looked as if he hadn't shaved that morning, but he was wearing a suit, shirt and tie, and obviously cared about his appearance. Neither he nor the general layout inspired Tansey with confidence.

"You'd better come inside," Bromley said, showing no surprise when Tansey explained their business.

He led the way into a small room

which with the presence of three people immediately became cluttered. He pulled out a chair for Tansey, knocked a couple of empty beer cans off a stool for Abbot and seated himself behind a desk as bare as that of the chairman of some major undertaking.

"Now, what is it you want to know, gentlemen?" he asked. "It's about a car of mine, isn't it?"

"It's about the Ford Escort you hired to a Professor Angus Luton approximately two weeks ago. You have a record of the transaction?"

"No."

"Why not? Mr Bromley, it's against the law for anyone in the car hire business to — "

"But I'm not in the car hire business, Chief Inspector. I run a petrol station and I buy and sell used cars. That Ford Escort you're on about is one I bought a couple of months ago. I sold it the day before yesterday — to a policeman. All fair and above board. I've got the paperwork to prove it."

"And prior to that you hired it to Professor Luton?"

"I *loaned* it to him, as I might to a friend."

"He was a friend of yours?"

"Chief Inspector, you know better than that." Bromley's grin made Tansey want to hit him. "I'd never seen the guy until last — last — " He studied the large girlie calendar hanging on the wall. "The Saturday before last."

"Go on," said Tansey. "What made you lend him a car?"

"I was sorry for him," said Bromley cheerfully. "It was like this, see. He arrived in a taxi and as soon as he'd been paid the driver hared off at once, leaving this chap stranded. In fact, the man had been done. He said he'd asked to be taken to a car hire firm, but in fact he'd been brought out here — to Cowley — a nice long trip from central Oxford — and dumped. He told me he was a Canadian professor on holiday in the UK, and I believed him. It was obvious he didn't know his way round."

"Did he give you any proof of identity? For instance, did he show you his driving licence?"

For the first time Bromley appeared

uneasy. "No, I don't think he did. The question never arose. But he was a fine driver. I could tell by the way he handled the car when he drove off, and he brought it back last Friday in perfect condition. He certainly hadn't had any kind of accident."

"What about insurance?"

"All the cars on the lot are covered for any driver. They have to be, else people couldn't take them for test runs. Chief Inspector, what is all this about?"

"Let me ask the questions, please, Mr Bromley."

In fact, Tansey was wondering what to ask next. He didn't trust Bromley. He was sure Bromley was hiding something, but it was difficult to know what it might be or how the man might have broken the law. He was certainly within his rights to 'lend' one of his cars, even to a stranger, and it would probably be impossible to disprove his story.

"I assume you were well paid for your kindness," he said.

"Yes, indeed." Bromley was relaxed again. "Mr Luton was very generous, and of course he insisted on putting down a large deposit before he borrowed the car."

Abbot coughed, and Tansey glanced at him. "Sir, I was wondering if the Professor had left anything in the Ford when he brought it back. A lady's handkerchief?"

"Ah yes," said Tansey, remembering that Hugh Cassidy had mentioned finding a handkerchief on the floor of the car when he was parking it the first Saturday that the Professor had arrived at Evenlode House. "Did he leave anything behind, Mr Bromley? People often do, I gather."

"A lady's hanky, yes, but that was all." Bromley was quite composed. "It was a pretty thing and I gave it to my wife. If you want, I'll fetch it. My house is just five minutes away. In the meantime — "

Bromley opened a drawer in his desk and produced some papers. "Here's the bumph on the Ford, including the name and address of the cop that bought it."

Tansey glanced through the documents while Bert Bromley went off, whistling. Abbot said, "You noticed that he had all this ready for us, sir."

"I did indeed, but that's not really surprising, considering that the police had been making inquiries about this car. I'd be prepared to bet that these papers are all in order, but I think his story about lending that car to Luton stinks — though I don't know what of." Tansey sighed. "We'll have to have the Ford examined, though I'm pretty sure it'll be a waste of time. As for his handkerchief — I'd forgotten about it. Clever of you to remember, Abbot."

"Thank you, sir, but I can't see it helping us much. It strikes me this Professor has gone out of his way to strew our path with puzzling but meaningless clues, as if he was playing some kind of game."

"I couldn't agree more," said Tansey. "If only we could find the damned man — But here comes the handkerchief, doubtless beautifully laundered. And, who knows, Abbot, it might bring us luck."

16

IT was the morning of the following day, and still early. Evenlode House was quiet. Most of the residents were in bed, or at least in their apartments. Dorothy Webb was fast asleep, exhausted, and in her sitting-room WPC Morton, who was up and dressed and had made herself a cup of tea, was wondering if she could risk having a cigarette. Anne Horne, who had been kept awake both by her arthritis and by worry about the situation at Evenlode, was soaking in a hot bath, and Kenneth Barnard was having his daily shower. But Norman Poynter, as was his habit, was solemnly swimming up and down the pool using his oldfashioned breast stroke. Outside, a couple of police officers patrolled the grounds, glad that the night had been dry and that their period of duty was nearly over.

The Cassidy 'family' was in the kitchen, having breakfast. It was not a cheerful gathering. They all looked tired, and even Patrick, who was renowned for his appetite, was eating with less than his usual enthusiasm. Hugh Cassidy had had no good news for them. The bank had refused to increase their loan. The insurance on Evenlode was due, and the premium had been trebled. As for the ludicrous offer that had been made for Evenlode, it was impossible to accept it, even if they had wished to do so.

"And we don't wish," Simon said firmly.

"But what else can we do?" Patrick demanded, his mouth full.

"Cut down on food," retorted Jill promptly.

Her husband gave her a fierce glance. "This is serious, Jill."

"Dear God, I know it is! Isn't there *anything* we can do, Dad?"

"Not much," said Hugh. "Not until we get rid of the police and can return to something like normality."

"We can try," said Lucinda with determination. "We must try. First, we've got to find a buyer for Mrs Luton's apartment. It's our one hope, but it's not going to be easy, with all the adverse publicity we're getting. However, would you agree that we set the price of the lease at no more than the amount we shall owe Mrs Luton's estate?"

"That means no capital profit on the last eighteen months. In fact, if you take inflation into account, it'll mean a dead loss," said Patrick.

They argued the point for a while but, as Hugh pointed out, they had very little choice. The first requirement was to pay off Mrs Luton's estate, and selling the apartment was the only means of doing that. If they failed to sell by the time prescribed by Mr Crewe, then they would face bankruptcy.

"But if we sell, even at a loss," Hugh said, "we cover our immediate money troubles, and we rekindle some kind of confidence among our present residents. That confidence is absolutely essential if we're to survive. And I don't have to tell you that this attack on Miss Webb has badly shaken what confidence did remain after Mrs Luton's death and the other misfortunes we've had lately."

"Has Miss Webb no idea why she was

attacked?" asked Val. "Did she see or hear anything, for instance?"

"No, she says not," replied Lucinda. "And it's not even as if her apartment was on the same floor as Mrs Luton's. Perhaps the intruder's crazy, but that doesn't help to reassure the residents. They feel they're sitting on top of a volcano that may erupt at any moment."

"Don't we all?" said Val.

"Well, *you* are quite free to leave Evenlode whenever you want, aren't you?" Sarah's voice was cool.

"I — I'm sorry. I didn't mean — " Val was taken aback.

"Sarah, that was a bloody nasty thing to say." Simon was angry.

Sarah looked at him and smiled. She didn't apologize. But Lucinda intervened, and what might have been an unpleasant quarrel was avoided.

★ ★ ★

Later in the morning Anne Horne lay on a lounger beside the swimming pool. It was a glorious day. The sliding roof and all the glass doors were open, and the scent of roses drifted in from the garden. There was no sign of the shambles the pool area had been a week or so ago and, except for the fact that there were fewer people about than usual, everything appeared normal.

"Not a policeman in sight," said Norman Poynter, putting down the two cups of coffee he was carrying on the table beside Anne, and seating himself. "It's really quite peaceful here, isn't it?"

"Yes, at the moment," Anne replied. "Norman, I was wondering if we could do something to help the Cassidys."

"Financially, you mean? I'm all for it, Anne, but what on earth can we do? We can't exactly pass the hat round, can we? It would be much too embarrassing for everyone. What do you think about it, Kenneth?" This to Kenneth Barnard, who had pulled up a chair and joined them.

"I must admit I'd been wondering if some kind of loan might be arranged," said Barnard. "We all know the terms of our leases. One of the main things Hugh Cassidy's got to do is find enough money to buy back the remainder of Morag's lease, and I bet his bank's turned him down."

"It would be an awfully bad investment, Kenneth," said Norman. "Almost an unsecured loan."

Anne intervened. "Personally, I was thinking more about finding a new resident to buy Morag's apartment."

"How would you propose we do that?" inquired Kenneth.

"Well, it occurred to me that between us, the residents, we must know a lot of people, and they have friends. It's not improbable that among them there's someone who would like to come to Evenlode. So if we spread the news — "

She stopped. The two men were shaking their heads. They didn't think her proposal was realistic. Kenneth brandished a newspaper, and she saw it was a copy of the *Colombury Courier*.

"What news, Anne?" he demanded. "Don't forget the present situation. The news is all about *Fortress* Evenlode, at any rate in this rag, and the others — the tabloids, at least — will be sure to pick it up. Our Mr Balham's excelled himself this morning. He makes the place sound like a Russian *gulag*. Personally, I think Cassidy could sue."

"What good would that do? It would only mean more unwelcome publicity." Anne Horne was tart.

"Of course it would," Norman agreed. "But, my dear, could you put your hand on your heart and recommend that in the present circumstances a friend — or a friend of a friend — should buy an expensive lease on an apartment here at Evenlode House?"

"I suppose not," Anne admitted reluctantly.

"It would be an absolute con, wouldn't it?" Kenneth said, amused that Anne Horne should contemplate such a move.

Kenneth exchanged glances with Norman, which Anne didn't fail to notice, and she guessed what they were thinking. She finished her coffee, then with an effort stood up quickly, waving to them to stay seated.

"I'll leave you now," she said. "Perhaps you'll come up with a better idea. I'm going to have a chat with Dorothy Webb."

Anne went along the corridor to the hall and, seeing Sarah at the reception desk, thought she should first ask if Dorothy was well enough to welcome a visit. Sarah was doing some embroidery and was obviously not busy. As Anne came across to her, she put down her work and smiled.

"Hello, Mrs Horne. How are you? How's the arthritis?"

"Hello, Sarah. I'm not too bad, thank you. What are you working on?"

"It's going to be a blouse when it's finished, but I've not got very far."

"What's that?" Anne pointed to a small metal object lying on the desk top.

"A needle-threader. This work's so delicate I have to use a very fine needle, and it takes ages and ages to thread the silk without that thing."

"A needle-threader?"

"Yes. Haven't you seen one before? People whose sight isn't too good often use them."

"I remember now. Miss Webb was complaining that she had to borrow one so as to be able to do some mending."

"It wasn't mine. It might have been

Lady Sarson's. I know she has one."

"Perhaps," Anne said and, as the telephone rang and Sarah reached to pick up the receiver, she added quickly, "I was going to ask you, is it all right if I pay a visit to Miss Webb now?"

Sarah nodded and, thoughtfully, Anne Horne went along to Dorothy Webb's apartment.

★ ★ ★

Chief Inspector Tansey and Sergeant Abbot arrived at Evenlode House later than they had intended. Tansey had been forced to face a press conference, which had been noisy and demanding and had badly delayed him. On their arrival they confirmed that the night had been uneventful and then, as a matter of courtesy, went to make sure that Miss Webb had not been disturbed.

They met Anne Horne as she was about to leave Dorothy Webb's apartment and, to Tansey's surprise, she asked him if he would spare her a few minutes before he left Evenlode that day.

273

"As soon as I'm free," he said. "Where will I find you?"

"I'll be in my apartment."

"Right," said Tansey, curious about what she wanted; Anne Horne was not someone to waste his time when he was on duty.

The call on Dorothy Webb was brief. It consisted of her assuring the two detectives that she had quite recovered from the attack made on her and that, in spite of much thought, she could conceive of no reason for it and was convinced it had been a mistake. She did not, however, suggest that WPC Morton should leave her and resume her normal duties.

Almost as an afterthought as they were leaving Tansey produced the handkerchief Bert Bromley claimed to have found in the car that he had 'lent' to Angus Luton. As expected, it had been washed and ironed by Mrs Bromley, but it had been identified by Hugh Cassidy as 'probably the same one' he had noticed when he parked the Ford for Luton on the latter's first visit to Evenlode.

Tansey suspected that it would prove

to be a worthless piece of evidence, but he couldn't afford to ignore it. He was not surprised when Miss Webb shook her head. It wasn't hers, and to the best of her knowledge she had never seen it before.

"But it might be Miss Field's," she added. "Sarah does a lot of embroidery."

When asked, however, Sarah denied ownership. "It most certainly is not mine," she said after the shortest of inspections. "I'm sure you don't mean to be insulting, Chief Inspector, but these so-called embroidered flowers in the corner were done by machine."

"I'm sorry. I didn't know." Tansey smiled ruefully.

"No. Why should you?" Sarah returned his smile. "Needlework is my hobby." She gestured to the blouse on top of the reception desk. "I regret to say it makes me snobbish about mass-produced objects like this."

"It must make you observant about them too. Please, Miss Field, have a good look at that handkerchief."

"Why?" Sarah began, and shook her head. "OK. I won't bother you with questions, and I'll make a guess. This handkerchief probably came from a box of half-a-dozen or so, and was given to someone as a present. It could belong to almost anyone." She hesitated and, giving the handkerchief back to Tansey, said. "You might try Valerie Rowan. Tell you what, Chief Inspector, if you go along to the small sitting-room I'll get her to bring you some coffee and you can ask her."

"Thank you. That would be fine," said Tansey.

"What do you think, sir?" asked Abbot as they went along to their interview room. "Does Miss Field really believe it might be Miss Rowan's handkerchief, or is she just being bitchy?"

"I'd say both, Abbot. She believes it's the sort of inferior object Miss Rowan might possess — and she is being bitchy."

★ ★ ★

Val Rowan made no attempt to deny it was her handkerchief. She had brought in a tray with coffee and a plate of biscuits and had put it down on a side table beside Abbot, who said he would cope with it. Then Tansey held out the handkerchief to her.

"Yes, it's mine," she said, surprised. "I didn't know I'd lost it. Where did you find it, Chief Inspector?" Her voice trailed away. Her first reaction had been one of complete innocence, until it seemed to strike her that something might be wrong, and she blanched. "I — I don't understand."

"It was found in the Ford Escort that Professor Luton drove on his visits to Evenlode House, Miss Rowan," said Tansey.

"Oh!" Val smiled crookedly. She appeared to be thinking. "Is that important?"

"I don't know," said Tansey. "Can you explain how it happened to get there?"

"Professor Luton gave me a lift once. It must have been then."

"When, Miss Rowan?"

"I — This is very embarrassing, Chief Inspector." Val bit her lower lip, her eyes wide. "It's also very silly."

"Please tell us, Miss Rowan — now! There's no need to be embarrassed."

"No, of course not. I'm being stupid." But Val was seemingly in no hurry to explain. "You see, it was like this. The Saturday before last I went into Oxford to visit a girlfriend, and I missed the bus I should have caught to get me back to Evenlode in good time to serve at Mrs Luton's party, which I'd promised to do. So I decided to hitch, though it's not something I make a practice of."

"And Professor Luton picked you up?" Tansey didn't bother to hide his disbelief.

"No, Chief Inspector!" Val said coldly. "An elderly couple took me as far as Colombury, and gave me a lecture on the dangers of hitch-hiking. From Colombury I started to walk to Evenlode. In fact, even then Professor Luton didn't 'pick me up', as you put it, Chief Inspector. He stopped and asked me the way to Evenlode House, and when I told him I was going there he naturally offered to give me a lift."

"I see," said Tansey doubtfully. "But why didn't you mention this before, Miss Rowan, and just what's embarrassing about it?"

"I didn't mention it before because — and this is the embarrassing bit — because of my — my position at Evenlode. Chief Inspector, I'm just a maid of all work here, and I'm grateful for the job. The Cassidys treat me as if I were a member of the family, but of course I'm not. However, some of the residents — not Mrs Luton, she was always very kind — but some of the others . . . Oh, I suppose you can't blame them. They're old and most of them have been used to having a bevy of servants at their beck and call, but . . . "

"Miss Rowan, what are you trying to say?"

"That I couldn't appear to be already on friendly terms with Professor Luton when I was the maid serving drinks and canapés, and the special guests Mrs Luton had asked to meet the nephew she was so proud of had never seen him before. Some of them — the more snobbish ones — might have been annoyed, affronted. Don't you understand, Chief Inspector?"

Tansey ignored the question. "So what did you do, Miss Rowan?"

"I explained the situation to Professor Luton as soon as he'd said who he was, and why he was going to Evenlode. He was very nice about it, though being a Canadian he thought it was a bit of a joke. But he dropped me at the end of the drive, and agreed to pretend not to have met me before. Anyway," she ended sadly, "that must have been how my handkerchief got in his car."

"Right, Miss Rowan," said Tansey dismissively. "Thank you for your explanation."

Val Rowan hesitated as if she expected the Chief Inspector to say something more. When he remained silent she gave a little bow of her head, and went. Reflectively Tansey watched the door close behind her.

"So what's your opinion, Abbot?" he inquired. "Did you accept her story?"

"It sounded reasonable, sir, but she made rather a mouthful of it."

"Hm-m, yes. Well, I think I'll keep an open mind for the moment, though I'm inclined to believe her." Tansey pushed back his chair and stood up. "I'll leave you to finish the coffee and biscuits now,

Abbot, and go and have a word with Mrs Horne."

"OK, sir. Let's hope she's got something for us."

★ ★ ★

Anne Horne greeted Tansey apologetically. She had had second thoughts and was wondering if she might be about to waste his time.

He reassured her. "My dear, it's often some seemingly insignificant fact that makes all the bits of the puzzle suddenly fit together."

But not this time, he thought, as an hour later and after another frustrating interview with Dorothy Webb, Abbot drove him away from Evenlode.

What Miss Webb had failed to mention to anyone, including Tansey, until Mrs Horne drew the information from her was that on the Saturday morning Morag Luton was killed, Dorothy had twice gone upstairs to Lady Sarson's apartment, which was along the corridor in the west wing quite close to Mrs Luton's. She had gone there first to borrow and then to return a needle-threader.

Anne hadn't questioned her. She had thought it best to leave this to Tansey, who was eventually more or less satisfied that he had extracted from Dorothy all that she knew, which in fact was very little.

Dorothy Webb, on her first trip upstairs, had seen Jill Donne delivering the post to the various apartments. Jill had stopped for less than half a minute to speak to Val Rowan who had come out of Mr Barnard's apartment. Where Val had gone next Dorothy didn't know, as she had been busy explaining to Lady Sarson her wish to borrow a needle-threader; it might have been to Mrs Luton's apartment, or it might not. There had been no one about when Dorothy left Lady Sarson's.

On Dorothy's second trip, to return the threader, she had seen Professor Luton standing outside Mrs Luton's apartment. He was still there when Lady Sarson had answered her door. Then he had looked around sharply, as if he had been startled by an unexpected sound. Having returned the loan, Dorothy had begun to move towards the lift, and she had expected him to join her, but he had turned away and gone through the door leading to the top of the stairs.

As Dorothy had said before, she had seen nothing untowards that morning and though, interestingly, she had confirmed what Angus Luton had told Sarah, she certainly hadn't helped to solve the problem of who killed Morag Luton.

17

THE dog was the first to give the alarm. He stopped so abruptly that the police officer who held his lead nearly fell over him. The handler, a young constable, cursed softly. The dog ignored him. Ears pricked, he stood stock still, emitting a low deep growl. This was their third night on guard duty at Evenlode House, and until now nothing had relieved the boredom.

The constable peered into the darkness and listened, but all he could see were deeper shadows, and all he could hear was a breeze sighing in the trees. Nevertheless, he trusted the dog more than he would have trusted another man.

"What is it, Rollo?" he hissed.

The Alsatian whined, then began to pull him forwards, and as they rounded the garage block he smelt what the dog had sensed and saw the glow ahead. Fire! The dog ran and he ran. This time they came to a halt together some twenty-five yards in front of the Evenlode guest house, which was already well alight.

Flames could be seen dancing in the downstairs windows. The officer immediately reached for the radiophone on his lapel to call Colombury police station. He knew that his colleague patrolling at the other end of the grounds of Evenlode House would also receive the call, and come running. Colombury station would contact the fire brigade, and their own Headquarters at Kidlington. But, even as he watched the growing fire and heard the sound of burning wood, he knew it was too late. By the time the fire service arrived from Colombury there would be no hope of saving the guest house.

But how could it have happened? Less than forty minutes ago he and Rollo had passed along this way. Everything had appeared normal, and the dog had shown no sign of suspicion. Yet since then a fire had started and gained hold in a modern building which, Dr Cassidy had told him, was at present empty.

There was a loud thud, an explosion. The dog-handler conferred for a moment with the other officer who had joined him; it was already obvious that fire extinguishers or relays of buckets of water would be pointless here. But the alarm had to be raised; the guest house was some distance from the main building and the wind was so light that the danger of the fire spreading from flying sparks was minimal, but the Cassidys might feel it their duty to evacuate everyone. In any case, windows were beginning to light up as residents sensed or smelt or heard what was happening. Once more the constable and his dog — Rollo seemingly reluctant to leave the excitement — ran through the darkness. As they went they heard behind them another explosion, louder than the last.

An hour later the scene was very different. The comparatively peaceful night had given way to bustle and organized confusion, as fire-fighters from the Colombury station struggled in vain to control the fire, which now burned even more fiercely. Water rose in arcs from their hoses, but had no effect. Spurts of orange flame shot from the melted windows of the guest house, and at irregular intervals there came the odd thud of yet another explosion. Police and ambulance men stood by, together with a group of spectators — the Cassidys and most of the residents, many of whom had taken the opportunity to dress.

"Back! Back!" shouted the fire chief.

Everyone shuffled back a few steps and a sigh went up as the roof of the guest house fell in with a great roar. Black smoke and flame billowed out into the night sky, and ash drifted in the wind. The residents began to move away, some worried, some thinking with pleasure of their beds. The spectacle was over. The cleaning up and the reckoning would come later.

★ ★ ★

"There's nothing you can do at present, sir," the fire chief assured Hugh Cassidy. "Better try and get some sleep. I'll leave an appliance and a couple of men behind to keep the house — or what remains of it — damped down, so as to make certain there's not another outbreak, and Sergeant Donaldson's promised to increase the number of men on guard. I'm sure you appreciate that no one should go near the place until it's cooled off and the official investigators have had a chance to examine it."

"Of course. I understand, and thank you for all your help."

"I wish we could have done more, but frankly there was no chance of the building not being gutted." He hesitated. "I take it you're insured, sir?"

"Oh yes. It could be worse," Hugh said, and added as he walked back to the main house with Lucinda, Simon and Val, "So *much* worse! Supposing some of the residents had had guests staying there. They'd have been incinerated. I'd never have forgiven myself."

"Hugh, for God's sake, you can't blame yourself for this."

"Yes, I can, Cindy. Oh, not for the fire. I didn't start the bloody blaze. But considering what's been happening to us recently I should never have stored the paint in there. It was asking for trouble."

"Dad, it was the obvious place," Simon protested. "After all, it was a guest house suite we were going to redecorate. At least we won't have to do that now."

"Hugh, from what you just said — you think the fire was started deliberately?" Lucinda was appalled.

"I don't know, Cindy. It might have been an electrical fault or something, I suppose. We'll have to wait and see. Let's forget it for the moment."

But Patrick was not so easily rebuffed. He was determined to discuss the matter at once. He was waiting with Jill and Sarah in the hall for the others to return, eager to know what had happened. They had stayed behind reluctantly, and only when Hugh had insisted that some of the family should be there in order to deal with any problems that might arise and to reassure any nervous residents.

"How bad was the fire?" Patrick asked.

"Complete. The whole place was gutted. The roof fell in and . . . " Hugh shook his head. "It's a mess."

"But it's fully insured?"

"Of course it's insured, Patrick, but not fully." Hugh was on edge and had no desire for an argument. "You know perfectly well that insurance never covers the whole cost of replacement."

"Especially furnishings and fittings," said Lucinda. "Costs will have risen, too."

Simon yawned. He was tired — they were all tired — and he sensed his father's impatience with Patrick. "Let's go to bed, or it'll be time to get up," he said.

"No, hang on a minute!" Patrick was not to be gainsaid. "This is important, hellish important! I've been thinking and — "

"Patrick's had a bright thought?" Jill said, unsure whether to take him seriously or not.

"Can't it wait?" Sarah had no such doubts; like Simon, she could foresee that the next twelve hours or so were going to try them all, and they needed to get some rest while they could.

"No! Don't you understand? Our immediate problem is solved. The guest house has been burnt down. We claim the insurance money, which is our right, and we use it to pay off the lease of Mrs Luton's apartment. Later, when we've sold the apartment again, we can rebuild the guest house."

Patrick was excited. He looked from one to another of them in triumph, expecting them to share his enthusiasm, but only Jill responded. The others were clearly doubtful.

"Well," Patrick said when no one spoke. "What do you think? Why shouldn't it work? It's a sensible arrangement, isn't it? Logical?"

"It's a possibility, Patrick," Hugh said at last. "No more than that. We mustn't count on it. Our insurance company is pretty fed up with us at present. You can't blame them. And this will be a huge claim. They'll almost certainly fight it."

"How?" Patrick couldn't hide his disappointment.

"They might try to prove negligence on our part and, if there's any question of the cause of the fire being arson, they'll delay without a doubt. What's more, we'll probably be the primary suspects and if they refuse to pay the claim or delay too long we'll be in deeper than we are at present. So don't let's kid ourselves that our troubles are over. There could well be worse to come."

There was silence as each of them absorbed Hugh's brutal words. Patrick, who had been most hopeful, was now the most despondent, but they were all depressed.

As usual, it was Lucinda who rallied them. "Come on, everyone," she said. "Bed! And cheer up! Our luck must change soon."

★ ★ ★

In the bright mid-morning sunshine the remains of Evenlode's guest house, a black and desolate ruin, smelling of smoke and damp wood-ash, made an unhappy picture. The police had cordoned it off to prevent any unauthorized person from getting too close, but the news had inevitably spread and outside the cordon cameras whirred and pressmen interviewed any resident willing to speak to them. The Cassidys and their staff were keeping well away. Inside the cordon Sergeant Donaldson was talking to a tall, authoritative man in a grey suit and through the glassless windows other figures could be seen picking their way carefully among the rubble as they sought the cause of the fire.

The arrival of Detective Chief Inspector Tansey, accompanied by Detective-Sergeant Abbot, caused a stir. The grey-suited man looked up with interest. Sergeant Donaldson hurried to greet his superior. The few remaining residents drew back, but the media men pressed forward.

"What can you tell us, Chief Inspector?"

"How did the fire start?"

"Give us a break, Chief Inspector?"

"Who's going to gain from the destruction of the guest house, Chief Inspector?" This last and leading question from Balham of the *Colombury Courier*.

Tansey waved a dismissive hand in the air. "If I could answer all your questions I needn't be here at all," he said. "Later! You probably know more than I do at the moment."

Somewhat officiously Sergeant Donaldson introduced the two detectives to the grey-suited man. Colin Dewhurst, a representative of the insurance firm with which the Cassidys dealt, proved to be a laconic character.

Having shaken hands, he said, "Arson, Chief Inspector. Clear case, cut and dried."

"There's evidence?" Tansey found himself speaking in the same clipped manner.

"Plenty. Cans of paint. Cleaning fluid. The owners say they were going to do a spot of redecorating, but . . . " He shrugged. "Water-sprinklers turned off, so my men tell me. I've two experts in there with the men from the fire brigade and your police."

They were not *his* police, Tansey thought. Strictly speaking, the fire, arson or not, was not his business — unless it was connected with Morag Luton's murder and the attack on Dorothy Webb. But he was interested in anything, especially anything unusual, that happened at Evenlode House.

"Have you any theories about it, Mr Dewhurst?" the Chief Inspector asked.

Dewhurst shrugged. "Gain or revenge."

"What?" This reply was a little too elliptic, even for Tansey.

"Just this. People burn down the

property of others out of spite, in which case we pay out, though we may sue later." Dewhurst gave a thin smile. "Or they burn down their own property — from greed or need — in which case, if it can be proved, we don't pay. It's as simple as that."

Tansey refrained from commenting that the insurance investigator was lucky; there *were* simple criminal cases, but he never seemed to get them.

"And in this instance?" he prompted.

"We'll be very careful before we settle the claim. Very careful," Dewhurst repeated with seeming satisfaction.

★ ★ ★

While he waited in the interview room for Abbot to fetch Dr Cassidy, Tansey considered the latest twist in the Evenlode saga. He did not believe that Hugh Cassidy had deliberately set fire to the guest house in order to get his hands on some ready cash, though there was no doubt that he needed money. The alternative, as suggested by Dewhurst, that someone had acted out of spite — or,

Tansey's own interpolation, to gain some advantage for himself — seemed by far the more likely explanation for all the recent happenings at Evenlode. But who? And why?

Tansey was no nearer finding answers to these questions, but with each incident his conviction grew that the individual or individuals responsible were closely connected to Evenlode House, or were aided and abetted by someone who was. Inside knowledge was apparent too often for it to be mere coincidence. And he wondered if it were conceivably possible that Morag Luton had chanced on the explanation, and that was the reason she had been killed.

The arrival of Abbot with Hugh Cassidy interrupted his thoughts, and for a while they discussed the destruction of the guest house.

"I agree it's a bad business," concluded Tansey quietly. "Is it a very bitter blow?"

"The death knell." Hugh's smile was grim. "At any rate if the insurance refuses to pay — and Dewhurst wasn't exactly sympathetic when I spoke to him earlier."

Before Tansey could comment there was a bang rather than a knock on the door, and simultaneously it flew open. Sergeant Donaldson burst into the room. His usual stiff, self-important manner had disappeared. He was red-faced and panting heavily as if he had been running, and he was clearly excited.

"Chief Inspector! They've found a body!" He paused to catch his breath. "In the ruins of the guest house. Horribly burnt, it is."

"Oh God!" Automatically Hugh Cassidy stood up. He was pale and he wetted dry lips with his tongue. "Who — ?"

"Impossible to say, but probably male."

"All right." Tansey took charge. "Go back, Donaldson. Tell them the body's not to be moved and — "

"It can't be, sir. There's a great beam fallen across it. It's going to be a job getting it free."

"I see. Well, I don't want *anything* moved until the scene of crime people get here. Understand?"

"Yes, sir."

Tansey reached for the telephone. "Abbot, you get Inspector Whitelaw on our car phone. He can organize his team. I'll call Dr Band from here, and get a pathologist, probably Ghent."

The two sergeants hurried out, but Hugh Cassidy lingered while Tansey telephoned. "Chief Inspector," he said when Tansey put down the receiver, "have you any idea who this — this could be? There's no one missing from Evenlode."

"It could be a tramp, who had just decided to spend the night in your guest house, Dr Cassidy," Tansey said slowly. "It could be the arsonist who got caught in his own fire. There's no point in guessing at this stage."

But Hugh Cassidy's remark that no one was missing from Evenlode had made Tansey remember that someone was absent who could be said to be connected with Evenlode — and that was Professor Angus Luton.

18

"WHAT can I tell you, Chief Inspector? Quite a lot, in spite of the fact that he was so thoroughly barbecued that his own mother wouldn't recognize him." Dr Ghent gave a self-satisfied smile. "You've already gathered he was male. A white man. Age somewhere around thirty to thirty-five. Five feet ten in height. Well built. Not fat, but an indoor rather than an outdoor type, I would guess from his probably flabby muscles. I wouldn't like to take a chance on his profession, but it wasn't manual work. He had taken care of himself, but he had poor teeth — could be the result of neglect in childhood. The dentistry — "

"Poor teeth?" Tansey was surprised.

Ghent raised his eyebrows inquiringly. "You believe you know who he is?"

Tansey was embarrassed. He had told no one of his suspicion that the burned corpse might be that of Professor Angus

Luton. Indeed, it could scarcely be called a suspicion — it was more of a hunch, perhaps — and now it looked as if he was going to be proved wrong. But he saw no reason why he should admit all this to Ghent.

"I was interested," he said. "Hopeful we might be able to trace him through his dentist."

"Could be, but don't count on it — and first find your dentist. Anyway, I'm not an expert, but I'd be inclined to believe that it was the work of more than one National Health practitioner. Maybe he moved around. Maybe none of them satisfied him, but he couldn't afford to go private. Who knows?"

"Thanks anyway," Tansey said, accepting that his hunch had merely been misleading. Canadian dentistry was among the best in the world, and a professional man like Angus Luton was not the kind of individual to neglect his teeth. "Anything else?"

"Cause of death was smoke inhalation, as you might expect. But he certainly wasn't a tramp having a kip down in an empty house. Nevertheless, regardless of whether he set the fire himself and got caught in it, I doubt if his reason for being in the Evenlode guest house was legitimate."

"Why do you say that?"

"Because of his clothes."

"Weren't they all burnt?"

"Not completely. For instance, scraps of material from the stocking mask he was wearing had stuck to his facial skin."

The pathologist grinned in triumph at Tansey's dumb-founded expression, but the Chief Inspector's amazement was not due to any admiration for Ghent's brilliance. He was recalling Miss Webb's description of the man who had climbed through the window of her apartment's sitting-room and tried to smother her. After his mistaken expectation that the incinerated body would turn out to be Angus Luton's he wasn't going to jump to any more conclusions, but that there could be two masked men wandering around Evenlode was surely overstretching coincidence.

And if this was true there was at least a connection, possibly indirect, between the killing of Morag Luton, which was linked to the attack on Dorothy Webb, and the various incidents seemingly designed to ruin Hugh Cassidy and his family.

★ ★ ★

The same afternoon Chief Inspector Tansey was sitting in his office, brooding. He could still see no pattern in the events at Evenlode. There remained too many unanswered questions. The most pressing seemed to be the identity of the man who had died in the guest house fire. If that could be discovered, Tansey thought, the rest might fall into place. But it was not going to be simple.

The other major question concerned Angus Luton. Either he was deliberately ignoring police requests to come forward, or he was no longer alive. By now the latter seemed the most likely choice since, in spite of his eccentric behaviour, he was a man of standing with a reputation to maintain and, in so far as it could be checked, he hadn't left Britain. Besides, he had told Sarah that he would be in touch, a promise he had failed to keep.

"Come in," Tansey said absently as there was a tentative knock on his office door. He had asked not to be disturbed, but he did not really regret the interruption; his ruminations had been getting him nowhere. "Come in!" he shouted when nothing happened.

The doubtful face of a WPC eventually peered round the door. "Sir, I — I'm sorry to disturb you, but there's a Mr James Crewe on the telephone, *demanding* to speak to you. He says it's vital and — and urgent. He was very — very aggressive."

"OK," said Tansey. "Put him through."

Tansey couldn't imagine the solicitor being aggressive, but he was wrong. Crewe was at the very least extremely determined, and he was agitated. He repeated that he had vital and urgent information, but he flatly refused to discuss it on the telephone.

"All right, Mr Crewe. I'll be with you in about half an hour."

Tansey was putting away his files and locking his cabinets when Inspector Whitelaw came in. "I won't keep you, sir," he said. "I just wanted to report that I've checked the possible 'missing persons' in the district and none of them seems to fit with the Evenlode corpse."

"Pity, but too much to hope, I suppose."

"I've also sent the relevant particulars to the Met, but it'll take longer to get results there as they have so many individuals listed as 'missing' in the London area. And I was wondering, sir, about Angus Luton. Do you think it would be worth while to have the mortuaries checked for unidentified bodies? After all, he should have turned up by this time if he's still with us."

"That's a good idea," Tansey agreed; he had considered it earlier, and had decided it was rather soon to make that sort of inquiry, but now . . . "Anything else?"

"For such as it's worth, I've heard a rumour that a new major road is likely to be cut through what is at present the grounds of Evenlode."

"Really? You might try to verify that, Inspector. There could be something behind it. At the moment I distrust anything that's even vaguely connected with Evenlode."

Whitelaw grinned. "Will do, sir."

★ ★ ★

"Come in, Chief Inspector. Come in and sit down." James Crewe offered Tansey his bony hand, then waved him to a chair. "As I indicated on the telephone, I have grave and serious information to impart to you, information which will be as much a shock to you as it was to me."

Tansey bowed his head in acknowledgement. He didn't speak, hoping to persuade the solicitor to get to the point as soon as possible.

"My information concerns Professor Angus Luton," Crewe continued rather pompously. "You — and to a lesser extent I — have been eager to get in touch with him since the death of his aunt, Mrs Morag Luton. At last I have located him. To be more precise he has located me. He telephoned me today from Vancouver, British Columbia, where he has been staying with friends."

"He's returned to North America?"

Tansey was surprised. All flights out of the United Kingdom had been checked for the name of Angus Luton, and the name had not been on any of the passenger lists. Passport control had been warned, but nothing had turned up. True, Luton could have taken a ferry to France and gone from there, but . . . Tansey concentrated on what Crewe was saying.

"Professor Angus Luton has not returned to North America, Chief Inspector, for the very good reason that he has never left North America this summer."

"What?"

"He has been on a bicycle trip by himself across the United States. His object was to 'get away from it all', and he seems to have succeeded." Crewe was becoming more human now that he had delivered his initial blow. "Apparently he knew nothing of his aunt's death — or the manner of it — or the troubles at Evenlode House until today, when he saw an air mail edition of *The Times* in his friend's house. Needless to say he was horrified to learn that he was wanted by the English police and he telephoned me at once."

Tansey, astounded, nodded his understanding. Crewe was right. It had been a shock. Indeed, he was still trying to assimilate the implications of what he had been told. The fact that the man Evenlode House had accepted as Angus Luton was an impostor explained the doubts about him voiced by Kenneth Barnard and Norman Poynter, and even Dorothy Webb.

But, Tansey's thoughts continued, his aunt, Morag Luton, who should have known him better than anyone, had never doubted him. Or had she? Was that why she had been killed? Suddenly Tansey remembered the letter from Canada that had arrived at Evenlode on the morning of Mrs Luton's death and had subsequently disappeared, perhaps destroyed.

Realizing that Crewe, appreciating his problems, was looking at him with sympathy, Tansey said, "I suppose Professor Luton didn't mention that he had written to his aunt recently?"

"No, he didn't." For some reason the

solicitor didn't seem surprised by the question. "But you can ask him that yourself. He had planned to put his cycle on the train and return to Ottawa by rail from Vancouver, but naturally his plans have changed. He's flying to England immediately and will come straight to Oxford. I am to book him a room at the Randolph. He will want to see you, Chief Inspector, just as much as you want to see him. I have explained to him that you are in charge of the inquiry into his aunt's death. Incidentally he has asked me to represent him in the UK, and therefore I must request that in all fairness to my client you do your best to clear his good name as soon as possible."

"Of course! Of course!" Tansey said absently; Crewe's observation seemed unnecessary, but there was no point in commenting.

"I appreciate that this impostor must pose more questions for you than he has answered," Crewe continued. "Chief Inspector, tell me, have you any idea how this man managed to take Professor Luton's place, why he did it, what he had to gain, who he is and what's happened to him?"

"I only wish I could answer all your questions, Mr Crewe," said Tansey. "I have various ideas," he added, thinking that it might help to clarify them if he discussed them with the solicitor, who in the circumstances had a right to be curious. "But they really are only possibilities. Do you want to hear them?"

"Please, yes, Chief Inspector. You never know. I might be able to make a suggestion."

"Well, first, how did he manage it? The facts are that he phoned Mrs Luton out of the blue, said he was in Oxford discussing the possibility of taking an appointment there for a while, and looked forward to seeing her. He visited Evenlode House only three times, the last time briefly. No one except Mrs Luton had ever met him before, but he bore a close resemblance to a studio portrait of Professor Angus Luton, and he was obviously able to pose as him. The resemblance must originally have been chance, but he may have taken steps to heighten it. As for his knowledge of Professor Luton, that,

I think, he learnt indirectly from Mrs Luton, who was proud of her nephew and talked about him a great deal."

"Indirectly?" James Crewe queried.

"Yes. Say, from someone who noticed the likeness between the photograph in Morag Luton's room and the impostor, and was able to coach him in his part from Mrs Luton's conversations. It must have been someone at Evenlode House, Mr Crewe. He couldn't have done it by himself."

"My goodness! Conspirators! I assume their purpose was to get money out of poor Mrs Luton?"

"The impostor did get a thousand pounds, and he probably hoped for more."

"But she was killed. Did he kill her? Why, Chief Inspector? Why on earth kill a goose that may lay golden eggs? It doesn't make sense."

"There's no evidence that it was he who killed her, Mr Crewe. I don't know, but I don't believe it's as simple as it might seem."

"But he did bolt, which is surely suspicious. You've no idea where he might be, have you?"

Tansey hesitated. "I could make a guess, but it would be no more than a guess."

"Please, Chief Inspector." Surprisingly James Crewe's eyes twinkled behind his half spectacles. "I would treat your guess in complete confidence."

"Well, my guess is that at the present moment he's not far from here — in the Oxford mortuary."

"The arsonist?" Crewe caught the point immediately. "Dear heavens! Some people do lead exciting lives."

"As to who he is, I've no idea, but I intend to remedy that as soon as possible. So, if you'll excuse me, Mr Crewe — "

"Of course, Chief Inspector. I mustn't keep you." But the solicitor appeared thoughtful.

"And you'll let me know when Professor Luton — the real Professor Luton — gets here?"

"Yes. Yes. Chief Inspector, one more point. You believe that Mrs Luton's murder and the various unhappy incidents that have occurred recently at Evenlode House are inextricably connected?"

"I'm convinced of it." Tansey had stood up; he was eager to get away.

"In that case, though it goes against the grain for a solicitor to break a confidence, I intend to do so. I appreciate that there would be no point in it if I didn't expect you to make use of the information, should it be relevant to your inquiries, but I trust you will respect the source."

"Yes, Mr Crewe, you have my assurance." Slowly Tansey sat down again; he wondered what was coming.

James Crewe formed a pyramid with his hands and regarded the Chief Inspector over it. "It has come to my knowledge — how is of no importance — that a consortium of four persons is extremely eager to buy up land which would include Evenlode House and the neighbouring estate."

"You mean Ashley Ormonde's place?"

"Oh no!" Crewe shook his head. "Mr Ormonde is a member of the consortium. The neighbour to whom I refer is on the other side of Evenlode. He's an old man and is willing to sell, but is dickering about the price. His acreage is small in comparison, but the whole thing would make a neat parcel if — and I stress the if — Evenlode House could be included in it."

"There's a rumour that a new road is to be built in that area."

"So I've heard, but personally I don't believe it. It would be a waste of money. It's not needed. No, there must be some other reason for them to want to buy."

"Who are the other members of this consortium, Mr Crewe?"

"A businessman called John Rayner, a friend of Ormonde's, is one. I don't know who the other two are, but I gather that Ormonde and Rayner are the main promoters of the scheme, whatever it is. And I must stress, Chief Inspector, that they are both men of reputable character. One could not imagine them being involved with murder or arson but — and now it's my turn to guess — it's possible they may have information or even suspicions which they would hesitate to volunteer."

"I understand. And thank you very much, Mr Crewe," said Tansey. "I hope and believe that the pieces of the puzzle are beginning to fall into place — and, who knows, these gentlemen may be able to provide some of the missing pieces. Anyway, I'll keep you informed."

19

THE garage in Cowley where the pseudo-Professor Angus Luton had supposedly hired his Ford Escort in which to visit Evenlode House, was shut. But Tansey had Albert Bromley's home address, and Abbot drove there in five minutes.

Tansey saw the lace curtain in the front room of the neat semi-detached twitch as Abbot continued to hold his thumb on the bell. Then Bromley opened the door. Behind him they could see a small boy clutching a sandwich. Bromley too was munching. He had changed out of his business suit, and his casual clothes were scruffy.

"Hello, Chief Inspector!" He exhibited surprise, but he was not convincing; clearly he had seen them through the window. "What can I do for you? Whatever it is, 'fraid it'll have to wait. I'm having my tea."

"We want to talk to you, Bromley. Now!"

"No, not now. Can't you see I'm eating?" Bromley had been shaken by Tansey's sudden aggressive attitude, so unlike his diplomatic approach the last time they had met, but he was trying not to show it. "I'll be through in half an hour."

"I said now, and I meant now, Bromley. Either in your house or you come with us to your garage. If you don't like either of those alternatives, you can have the police station."

"But why? What for? What am I meant to have done? Are you charging me with anything?"

"Not yet, but obstructing the police in the course of their duties might do — for a start."

As Bromley stared at them a woman's voice called shrilly from the rear of the house. "What is it, Bert? Who is it?"

"It's OK, Marge. I've got to go out for a bit. It's a job. Shan't be long," Bromley answered and added, "I hope."

"Your garage, then?" Tansey said.

"Don't have much choice, do I?" Bromley scowled at the Chief Inspector and mumbled under his breath, just loud enough for Tansey to hear, "Fucking Gestapo, that's what you are."

They drove the short distance to the garage in silence. Bromley produced his keys and let them into the office, which appeared unchanged from their previous visit. But on this occasion Tansey seated himself behind the desk and motioned to Bromley to pull up a chair in front of him. Abbot found a stool and ostentatiously produced his notebook.

"Right!" Tansey said. "The last time we were here you told us a pack of lies about lending a car to a Professor Luton. So, let's start again — with the truth."

"I don't know what the trouble is, Chief Inspector. This bloke turned up. I lent him a car — hired it, if you like — and he brought it back. What he did with it in the meantime was his business. And that's all I've got to say."

"Oh no, it's not, Bromley!" Tansey smiled unkindly. "Your story always smelt, but we gave you the benefit of the doubt. Now we know better. First, this bloke didn't arrive in a taxi. Did he, Sergeant Abbot?"

"No, sir. We checked. No taxi," said

Abbot. He glanced at the Chief Inspector; he had never known a police officer with a greater facility for bluffing.

"Because he came on a motorbike, didn't he, Bromley?" This was a guess on Tansey's part, but the man who had tried to kill Dorothy Webb had probably been riding a motorbike. When Bromley didn't answer he repeated his question, "Well, didn't he?"

"I don't know why you should think that?" Bromley was obviously shaken.

Tansey, sure now that he had been right, pressed home his advantage. "And of course he never told you he was Professor Angus Luton, did he? What would be the point when he was an old mate of yours?"

Bromley saw what he thought was a chance. "How did I get hold of that name, then? Old mate, that's a laugh! I'd never seen the bugger before in my life."

Tansey sighed. "When he returned the car he told you what he'd been up to, conning an old lady that he was her nephew from Canada, but he said there'd been a spot of trouble — she suspected

318

him — and he'd had to clear out. And you agreed to cover for him, didn't you, Bromley? Isn't that the truth?"

"No, it isn't!"

"Did he tell you what his spot of trouble was?" Bromley glared at Tansey and didn't answer.

Tansey smiled. "But we know what it was, don't we, Sergeant Abbot?"

"Murder, sir. Cold-blooded murder of a frail old lady," Abbot answered on cue.

Bromley had gone white beneath his tan. "I — I don't believe it. Nige would never — I don't believe it."

"Well, you'd better believe it, Bromley, because Nige has landed you in it up to the neck," said Tansey. "In fact, in the old days, before they abolished capital punishment, it might have been literally your neck. Even today you can get a pretty long stretch as an accessory to murder."

"But I'm not! I didn't! I knew nothing about it."

Tansey shrugged. "Why should we believe you, Bromley? All you do is tell us lies."

"Of course, if he chose to help us, sir — told us everything he knows about Nige — it might make a difference, mightn't it?" Abbot asked blandly.

"Yes, it might," Tansey agreed. "If he cooperated fully I expect it would."

Bromley had began to sweat, but still he hesitated, running a finger round the neck of his none too clean shirt. Then: "I will. I will, Chief Inspector. Cooperate, I mean. Trouble is, I don't rightly know that much."

"Try!" Tansey said, thankful that Bromley had broken; he didn't like bullying suspects, but sometimes it was necessary. "Tell us about Nige."

"Well, of course his real name isn't Nige, but you knew that and . . ."

They had not known it, nor quite a lot more that Albert Bromley had to say, but they showed no gratitude for the information that poured from him. Terry Trent, who had posed as Professor Angus Luton, was Nige's real name. Trent had not considered that Terry suited him and had renamed himself Nigel, inevitably shortened to Nige. He was, according to Bromley, something of a con man, always ready to turn a dishonest penny, but strictly small time.

"I can't imagine him trying to kill anyone, Chief Inspector," Bromley said earnestly. "Truly I can't. He isn't tough — more sly, like. I think if he did try a — a murder, he'd probably make a mess of it."

Tansey thought of Dorothy Webb. "Anything else?" he asked.

"Not really. I didn't know him very well, as I say."

"Well enough to lend him a car — a relatively new car, in good condition."

"He did me a favour once, so I owed him, and it seemed a harmless enough way of paying him back."

"OK." Tansey didn't bother to inquire about the nature of the favour. "Go on. Where did he live?"

"He lived with his sister, Mrs Green, when he was in Oxford, but he came and went. I hadn't seen him for over a year when he turned up that day."

Bromley produced Mrs Green's address, but couldn't remember the phone number. "Don't forget he left a deposit on the car when he took it," he added, "and he was flush. I saw his wallet. He was well dressed, too. I made a crack about it and he said he had a swell job at the moment working for a couple of gents, and he hoped that one good thing was going to lead to another."

"Let me get this straight," said Tansey, who had not been surprised to learn that Trent's sister was a Mrs Green; he remembered Inspector Whitelaw mentioning the name when he was checking up on the inhabitants of Evenlode House. "Trent was flush *before* he borrowed your car?"

"That's right. I gathered what he was up to next was something different." Bromley shook his head nervously. "I — I still can't believe in a murder."

"Did Trent have a girlfriend?" asked Tansey suddenly.

"Lots. Nige was always one for the girls, but he did hint there was someone special at the moment. He didn't say who. He wasn't here long, neither time, and I suppose he had other things on his mind besides tarts."

"What about his motorbike? Did you

keep it for him while he had your car?"
Abbot asked.

"No. The Escort was a hatchback and the bike fitted in easy. It was only one of those mopeds."

Bromley got out a handkerchief and mopped his face, which was wet with perspiration; Abbot's intervention had made him even more uneasy. "And that's it, Chief Inspector. I swear to God I know nothing of what Nige was doing while he had the car — or what he planned to do. He didn't confide in me — and I was certainly no accessory to anything."

"Right, Bromley. This time I believe you, so we'll be off. Now, listen! Be at the Headquarters of the Thames Valley Police in Kidlington tomorrow morning at eleven. Ask for me. If I'm not there someone else will deal with you. We'll have a typed statement of what you've told us this evening ready for you to read and sign. Understand?"

Bromley nodded. "Will — will that be all?"

"You may have to give evidence in court later, but that'll be all for now."

"Thank you," Bromley said weakly. "Thank you, Chief Inspector."

★ ★ ★

"And from here, sir?" Abbot asked as they did up their seat belts.

"We'll pay a call on this Mrs Green."

"Yes, sir." Abbot swallowed his hopes of getting to a meal that hadn't been reheated, and a wife who was making a great effort to restrain her irritation at his constant unpunctuality.

"This motorbike — moped, Abbot. If it was Nige who used it to get to Evenlode for his arson attack on the guest house, where is it now?"

Negotiating the traffic through Oxford, Abbot allowed himself the privilege of not replying. Anyway, it seemed to be a rhetorical question, albeit an important one, as Tansey didn't appear to expect an answer.

"Here we are, sir," Abbot said at last. "This is the Greens' place — at least it's the address that Bromley gave us."

Abbot had turned into the driveway of a tall Victorian house in North Oxford.

He drew up in front of the steps and, as Tansey got out of the car, he could see the many bellpushes with names beside them at the side of the front door, indicating that what had once been home to a large family was now a collection of small flats. Apparently the Greens lived in the basement.

Standing outside, the two officers could hear from that basement voices raised in anger, a man's and a woman's. However, when Abbot pressed the bell, there was immediate silence. They waited, and Abbot was about to ring again when the door was flung back on its hinges.

A small, irate man, going bald, regarded them with some hostility. "Yes. What is it? If you're Jehovah's Witnesses we're not interested."

"Police," said Tansey, as Abbot stifled a guffaw at the man's suggestion. "Detective Chief Inspector Tansey and Detective-Sergeant Abbot." He produced his warrant card. "We're making inquiries about a certain Terry Trent."

"I might have known it," the man said bitterly, losing little of his aggressiveness.

"You'd better come in." He showed them into a kitchen cum living-room but didn't ask them to sit down. "This is Mrs Green." He indicated a woman at least ten years younger than himself. "Police! Inquiring about your Nige, *dear*."

"Has he — has he had an accident?"

But Mrs Green was not nearly as naïve as her question suggested, Tansey thought cynically. If one of the Greens was in collusion with Terry Trent he would bet on it being the wife. "You're Terry Trent's sister, Mrs Green?" he said.

"Yes, that's right. His only relative, in fact."

Tansey glanced at Abbot, who produced a copy of Morag Luton's photograph of her nephew, Angus. "Is that him, Mrs Green?"

She frowned at the print. "Could be. Yes, it could be Nige. I've not seen this one, but . . . What's happened to him? You haven't told me." At least her anxiety was genuine.

"What you should be asking, girl, is what he's done," her husband said brutally. "What's he wanted for this time?

326

That would be more like it."

"When did you last see him?" asked Tansey.

"Saturday evening. He had supper with us. Then later he went off on his motorbike. I've not seen him since. He didn't come home. I looked in his room early the next morning and his bed hadn't been slept in."

"Is he in the habit of going off like this?"

"No! He may turn up unexpectedly, but he always tells me before he goes." Mrs Green was obviously worried. "Chief Inspector, do you know where he is, what's happened to him?"

"P'haps he's in gaol," Green said hopefully.

"He may have been involved in a fire." Tansey was picking his words with care.

"You mean he set fire to somewhere?" said Green.

"You don't sound surprised, Mr Green."

"I'm not. He burnt down half his school once."

"Steve! That was years ago. He denied it, and the police never proved anything.

He hasn't got a record — not like some!" Mrs Green was angry now, and her last remark served to silence her husband.

She turned to Tansey. "Chief Inspector, I don't care what he's done. He's still my kid brother. What's happened to him? Tell me! It's my right to know."

"Mrs Green, we're not sure, but it's a possibility that your brother's dead. A badly burned body was found in a fire that gutted the guest house of Evenlode House, some way out of Oxford, in the small hours of Sunday morning. So far the man hasn't been identified, but we believe he could be your brother."

"Oh God! No!" Mrs Green sat down heavily.

"Do you — do you want us to identify him?" Green didn't much like the idea.

"It may not be necessary," Tansey prevaricated. "Did Trent have a local dentist?"

"Actually he went to one a few weeks ago. A Mr — Mr — I've forgotten the name. Charged a hell of a lot too, and that was only the first appointment, but Nige said he was fed up with the

National Health and was going to get his teeth fixed properly."

"The bill's probably in Nige's room," Mrs Green said sadly; she looked miserable, but she wasn't crying.

"We'd like to examine his room," Tansey said, thinking that the pathologist had been right about the burned man's teeth.

"All right." She sighed. "I'll show you."

The room was small and too full of furniture. It held a three-quarter bed with a duvet, a chest of drawers and a cupboard. There was a scrap of carpet on the linoleum floor, and a poster on the wall behind the bed. But in the cupboard and the chest of drawers was a selection of clothes, most of which looked new and expensive; some were women's. Tansey held up a pretty blue dress.

"That belongs to Nige's whore," said Green, who had followed them to the room and was standing in the doorway.

"Don't call her that!" his wife said. "He was in love with her. He wanted to marry her."

"Besotted, more like," Green grumbled. He thought for a moment, then went on, "Funny, though. Nige never had any trouble getting girls to fancy him, and usually he took them for granted, but it's true he really went for this one. He'd have done anything for her — including paying a horrid price to get his teeth fixed."

"And did this girl return his affection?" Tansey asked.

"Yes. Yes, she did," said Mrs Green, perhaps a little too quickly. "I told you they were planning to get married."

"So you did," said Tansey. "Well, let's hope for her sake and yours that we're wrong and the chap who died the other night wasn't Nige."

"But we're damn sure he is, Abbot," said Tansey as shortly afterwards, having found and given a receipt for the dentist's bill and a wad of hundred-pound banknotes discovered under a loose floorboard, they left the Green's flat.

"Damn sure, sir," Abbot agreed. "Where now? Evenlode?"

"No. It's too late. I don't think she'll

try to scarper, but we'll warn our men on duty there."

"Poor girl," Abbot said. "I wonder how she got involved with Nige."

"Probably met him at a disco." Tansey had no sympathy to waste on Val Rowan.

20

BY now Tansey thought he knew most of the answers. And, without sympathy, he confronted Valerie Rowan across the table in the so-called interview room at Evenlode House — a room which he hoped would soon be restored to its normal purpose as a second smaller sitting-room for the residents.

Valerie Rowan wept. Tears streamed down her pretty face and her body shook with sobs. Tansey, ignoring Abbot's reproachful glances, waited. WPC Morton, no longer guarding Miss Webb, poured Val a glass of water and took it to her.

Val, who had been stunned when she had been given the routine caution that she did not have to say anything, but what she said might be given in evidence against her, had broken down completely when she had been forced to accept that the police knew of her relationship with Terry Trent, better known as Nige — and, what was more, that Nige was dead.

She made one piteous inquiry. "Are you sure it was Nige who was burnt to death in the guest house, Chief Inspector?" she asked.

"Quite sure!"

Earlier that morning, Inspector Whitelaw, with his usual efficiency, had arranged for the record of Trent's dentistry to be compared with that of the corpse. And, angry with himself for not having thought of the arsonist's need for a means of transport, had instituted a search at first light, which had uncovered Nige's moped and helmet hidden in a ditch not far from the gates of Evenlode.

"You had no previous knowledge that Trent intended to burn down the guest house?" Tansey asked.

"No, Chief Inspector! No! I'd have tried to stop him. Oh God! Nige was mad. I — I did my best to make him be sensible, but he wouldn't listen." Val had recovered her composure.

"I see. Now, let's start at the beginning. First, you tricked Simon Cassidy into taking you to Evenlode House. That supposed accident in Oxford was a put-up job, wasn't it? Why did you do it? What gave you the idea?"

"Nige was given money and promised more if we could make things go wrong at Evenlode, so that the Cassidys could be persuaded to sell, and we were tempted . . . "

Val admitted to setting up the Wilson girl as a thief by planting various objects (including Norman Poynter's wallet which she had found down the side of an armchair) in Zena Wilson's hold-all, and to putting paradichloro-benzine — provided by Nige — into the mushroom and veal casserole so as to make several of the residents ill. Nige, she said, had destroyed part of Evenlode's stone wall with a lorry, and later vandalized the swimming pool area. He had also planned to pull down the elm tree, but the storm had done it for him; so of that at least he was innocent, Tansey thought, in spite of Dr Cassidy's vague suspicions. Setting fire to the guest house had been his last violent act.

"Oh, I know it was wrong, Chief Inspector," Val continued. "I knew it from the start, but Mr Ormonde — " At this name Tansey looked up sharply. "Yes, Mr Ormonde, the Cassidys' neighbour," Val continued. "He was prepared to pay so much, and we needed the money. We were hoping to get married and now Nige . . . Nige . . . He was mad and he's paid for it." Again tears filled her eyes.

"For some of it," Tansey corrected her coldly. "He's left you to pay for the rest. What's more, Miss Valerie Rowan, causing wanton material damage is bad enough, but murder and attempted murder are vastly more serious matters."

Val stared at him in apparent dismay. "I don't understand, Chief Inspector. What's that to do with me?" She looked as if she were about to start to weep again. Abbot shuffled in his seat, but Tansey ignored him. WPC Morton brought another glass of water, but was rebuffed.

Tansey ignored Val's question, and seemed to change the subject. "Let's get to the impersonation of Professor Angus Luton. How did that come about?"

Val had grown calm again. "All right, Chief Inspector. I suppose I'm partly to blame for that," she said. "There was this photograph of Angus Luton in Mrs Luton's room. The likeness to Nige was striking, and Mrs Luton was always talking about her nephew, so I learnt a lot about him. I mentioned to Nige as a joke that he could be Luton's brother and — and he saw the possibilities. To him she was a rich old woman, ripe for the picking. But she was kind to me, just as the Cassidys were. Oh, I don't expect you to understand — of course I shouldn't have agreed, but I was in love with Nige, and the money he hoped to get from her would have really set us up. So I went along with him."

"Even so far as killing an old woman who had been kind to you?"

Val shook her head violently. "No! No! But once Nige had done it, what could I do? He threatened me, said he'd blame me, that if I didn't do exactly what he told me he'd throw acid in my face. And he would have, too. He'd really gone round the bend by then."

"Exactly why did he kill Mrs Luton?"

"Because of the letter from her nephew in Canada, which arrived that Friday morning. It was obvious from what the real Angus Luton had written that he wasn't in England, so Nige had to be an impostor. She was going to call the police there and then and have Nige and me arrested."

"Both of you?" Tansey expressed surprise. "You were in the apartment at the time?"

"No, of course I wasn't! Nige told me afterwards. He said that the old — that Mrs Luton guessed it was me who'd been feeding him information about her nephew and — and Nige acted on impulse. It wasn't premeditated."

"I see. And what did he say about Miss Dorothy Webb?"

"What he told me was that she was standing in Lady Sarson's doorway and she must have seen him come out of Mrs Luton's apartment, though he'd had to tell Sarah Field he'd not been inside. Anyway, he didn't kill Miss Webb and, as it turned out, either he'd been wrong or she didn't remember noticing him, so it didn't — "

"Didn't matter? Is that what you meant to say?"

Val shook her head. "By now I don't know what I meant to say, Chief Inspector. I'm confused. I feel ill and I — I'm frightened. What's going to happen to me?"

"WPC Morton will help you pack a bag. She'll accompany you to Headquarters, where you'll be asked to read and sign a typed statement containing the information you've just given us. You'll have an opportunity to contact your lawyer, or if you don't have a lawyer, one will be provided."

"You mean you're arresting me?" Val looked overcome.

"The formal arrest will take place at Headquarters, but in effect yes." Tansey's voice was expressionless.

★ ★ ★

Minutes after the departure of WPC Morton with Val Rowan the door of the interview room was flung open, and an irate Simon Cassidy came in. He hadn't knocked, and Tansey regarded him inquiringly.

"Yes, what is it, Mr Cassidy?"

"You've arrested Val. She wasn't able to tell me what she's meant to have done before that policewoman hurried her off, but it's absurd, Chief Inspector. She — "

"Mr Cassidy, it is not absurd! I have my Chief Constable's approval for the arrest, and a warrant will be ready at my Headquarters. If you'll forgive me for saying so, you have no idea what you're talking about."

It was Tansey's tone of voice rather than his words which set Simon aback. He glared at the Chief Inspector. In his agitation he was breathing fast.

"Please fetch your father, and I will explain the circumstances of Miss Rowan's detention to you both," Tansey said quietly.

"Dad's coming," said Simon. "I asked Sarah to fetch him."

"Good. Sit down, then."

Simon sat. Tansey, aware of the young man's attachment to Val Rowan, appreciated his distress but took care not to show his feelings. Luckily they'd didn't have long to wait. Dr Cassidy appeared almost at once, looking anxious. But, as Tansey gave them an abbreviated account of Nige Trent's activities, Hugh's anxiety was replaced by amazement and anger.

Simon, for his part, appeared more concerned with the role that Val Rowan had played. "She must have loved this Nige very much to go along with it," he said dismally, "especially after Mrs Luton was killed."

Hugh Cassidy stared at his son in exasperation. "Val Rowan, it seems, was fully prepared to get the Wilson girl sacked for thefts she hadn't committed and to poison half the residents of Evenlode. Dorothy Webb was extremely ill as a result of eating that casserole. She might easily have died. And if you're suggesting Val was acting in any manner other than reprehensibly, you're a fool, Simon."

He turned to Tansey. "I can understand that the impersonation of Professor Angus Luton was a bit of private enterprise on the part of this despicable pair, but I don't understand who put them up to making these attacks on Evenlode in the beginning, and why whoever that was should want to force me to sell."

"I can't answer that at the moment," Tansey said, "but I hope to do so quite soon. Meanwhile I'd like to speak to Miss Webb and Lady Sarson if convenient, here in this room, together or separately. I won't keep them long."

"Right, Chief Inspector." Hugh Cassidy looked at his watch. "The ladies will probably be in the drawing-room at this time. I'll ask them to come. Anything else? What about lunch?"

"If Mrs Cassidy would be so kind — just for one only. Sergeant Abbot will be returning to Headquarters with WPC Morton and Miss Rowan." Tansey thanked the foresight that had made him come to Evenlode in his own car and request Abbot to bring Morton. "Meanwhile — "

It was a signal of dismissal. The two Cassidys, still half-shocked by what they had just learnt, departed. A disgruntled Abbot, having received his orders but been deprived of his lunch, went off to collect WPC Morton and Val Rowan. Tansey, pleased with his morning's work, settled down to the telephone and to await the arrival of Lady Sarson and Miss Webb.

They arrived as he replaced the receiver, and he couldn't help but think what contrasting impressions they would make on a jury, the flamboyant Melissa Sarson with her jewellery and excessive make-up, and the dowdy, colourless Dorothy Webb. But Miss Webb, keeping more to the point than usual, repeated the evidence she had given before — essentially that she had seen no one emerge from Mrs Luton's apartment, that the Professor had rung the bell and had turned away sharply towards the stairs when there was no answer. Her version of events was confirmed by Lady Sarson, who had been glancing down the corridor over Miss Webb's shoulder. Tansey was well satisfied.

* * *

After an excellent lunch Chief Inspector Tansey drove himself to Auburn Manor, the home of the Cassidys' neighbour, Ashley Ormonde. He had said on the phone that his business concerned Terry

Trent, a man known as Nige, and was urgent. Ormonde had agreed to see him at two-thirty that afternoon.

On his arrival at Auburn Manor, an imposing house built over a hundred years ago of Cotswold stone, Tansey was shown by a maid into a book-lined room, too small to be described as a library, but comfortable in the style of a smoking-room in a superior London club. Ormonde rose to greet him, but didn't offer to shake hands.

"Sit down, Chief Inspector, and tell me why you wish to see me."

Tansey was not impressed by Ashley Ormonde's dictatorial manner. Ormonde, with his crest of white hair, red face and bulbous eyes, reminded Tansey of some strange kind of cock bird, a comparison strengthened by the way he held himself, as if he were about to strut across the room. But obviously the man was nervous — and with reason, Tansey thought. Ormonde was no fool; he knew full well that he was in deep trouble.

"Sir, I told you my business concerned Mr Terry Trent, your employee, otherwise known as Nigel Trent or Nige."

"I wouldn't call him an employee, Chief Inspector."

"Mr Ormonde, Trent is dead. He was burnt in a fire that he started himself in the guest house of your neighbours at Evenlode. But his girlfriend, Valerie Rowan, has been taken into custody. She has accused him of murder. Need I say more?"

"Murder? You mean Mrs Luton? But why on earth should Trent — "

Tansey told him, and it was apparent that Ormonde had had no idea of Trent's impersonation of Angus Luton. But he was quick to grasp the implication — that he bore a heavy moral responsibility and, for all his faults, he was appalled.

"It's dreadful!" he said. "Dreadful! I was aware that Trent was going too far with the incidents he and his girl were causing, but as long as they compelled Cassidy to sell Evenlode I didn't want to know any more. But to kill that little woman . . . I read about it, of course, but it never occurred to me to connect it with Trent. I can't imagine him . . . Thank God he didn't succeed in killing the other one, Miss Webb."

"Why was it so essential that Dr Cassidy should sell?"

"Money — my need of it. That was my only reason."

"I don't understand."

"No, you wouldn't, Chief Inspector." There was a touch of Ormonde's old arrogance. "But what with the recession and some bad investments, I'm almost on the rocks. Even if this deal had gone through I would have needed to go carefully until I'd recouped my losses. As it is — "

"What deal? You don't mean a road through these properties, do you? We've checked with the Ministry and it's a baseless rumour, sir."

"Of course! That was a red herring to draw attention away from our real plan."

"Which was?"

"My friend, John Rayner, is in the property market, and he's been asked by a wealthy client to find a parcel of land that would be suitable for a theme park. If we could have joined my estate to Evenlode and that of another neighbour who's already agreed to sell, we'd have had a perfect property. My daughter's getting married again, and my wife and I want to move into a smaller place nearer London, anyway. And if we could have got Evenlode cheap, we'd have made a killing." Ormonde coughed to cover his unfortunate choice of word.

"I see," said Tansey, thinking that it was just for this that two people had died, and nearly a third, that Rowan would go to prison and that the Cassidys had been given weeks of desperate anxiety. "But earlier, sir, you said you were broke. How did you stake Trent and his girlfriend?"

"I said almost broke, Chief Inspector — and those sums were peanuts. For the rest — to pay for my part in the deal — I intended to put up my house as collateral, and Rayner found two other chaps to make up a consortium. Incidentally, neither of them knows anything about Trent."

"But Mr Rayner knew and agreed to the plot?"

"Yes." Ormonde hesitated. "Chief Inspector, I'm not trying to put all the blame on John. I accept my full share — but I do believe he gave Trent too much encouragement."

"Well, I expect it will be up to the courts to decide, sir." Tansey stood up. He'd had enough of Ashley Ormonde, and saw no reason why the man shouldn't worry about consequences, as he had made the Cassidys worry. "I shall have to discuss with my superiors the possibility of a criminal prosecution for conspiracy, but, frankly, if you take my advice, you'll get in touch with your lawyer as soon as possible."

★ ★ ★

Chief Inspector Tansey gave the same advice to the Cassidys off the record before driving himself back to Headquarters. As the Chief Constable agreed when they were discussing the case later that day, quite apart from a criminal case, the Cassidys had every right to institute civil proceedings not only to recoup their material losses, but to seek compensation for mental suffering and harm done to the reputation of Evenlode House.

"Most of that should be simple and straightforward . . . " Midvale shifted his bulk in his chair. "I'm not so sure about what to charge Miss Rowan with. I should like to go for murder, or conspiracy to murder, but . . . You say Miss Webb won't be a good witness?"

"No, I didn't quite say that, sir. She waffles, but she doesn't contradict herself. And Lady Sarson is prepared to swear that what she saw from the doorway of her apartment when Miss Webb was returning the needle-threader confirms Miss Webb's evidence. It's clear that Trent did not go into Mrs Luton's apartment that Friday morning. Therefore he didn't kill her. So who did? To my mind, there's no doubt that Val Rowan was the murderer, for the reasons she ascribed to Nige. I believe she waited for him, out of sight at the top of the stairs, and told him to make an excuse for leaving Evenlode. She wanted to involve him and make sure that he, not she, would look guilty. Later, because she believed Miss Webb was a threat to her, she persuaded him, besotted as he was with her, to try to kill Dorothy Webb."

"All right, Chief Inspector, charge Rowan with murder, and we'll see what the Crown Prosecution Service has to say."

"Thank you, sir," said Tansey. It had been a long but satisfying day. And he was looking forward to lunch tomorrow with Mr James Crewe — and the genuine Professor Angus Luton.

The Third Letter

As from — Evenlode House,
Evenlode,
Oxfordshire.
October 25th 199-

MY dear Dick,
I am at present spending an enjoyable holiday with friends in Scotland and thought I would bring you up to date with events at Evenlode, which, thanks to you, is slowly becoming again the pleasant and peaceful haven it used to be.

We are no longer front page news. That nasty young man, Michael Balham, has been forced to apologize for the horrible things he wrote in the Courier and the little publicity we get now is good. I suppose there'll be another spate when Val Rowan is brought to trial for killing poor little Morag but it cannot reflect upon the Cassidys, who showed the girl nothing but kindness.

350

Her arrest was a bitter blow to Simon, but he seems to be getting over it and accepting that she never cared for him. Luckily Sarah is both sensible and forgiving and I have every hope that before too long he'll ask her to marry him, so that she'll be a real member of the 'family', which incidentally is going to have an addition. Jill and Patrick are expecting a baby early in the New Year.

Everyone is very busy. The guest house is being rebuilt. The Cassidys received a substantial sum from Ashley Ormonde and John Rayner in damages — as you'll know, the case was settled out of court — for all they had endured because of the conspiracy. So, financially, Evenlode is in good shape again, especially as a friend of Mr Crewe, a retired General, has bought Morag's apartment. He's a delightful man and fits in well here.

One other item. The Wilsons are back. Dr Cassidy insisted on paying them for the time they were away and added a nice extra bonus for the false accusation, though he wasn't to blame. Anyway, they are very happy and so are we.

And that's all my news. I shall return

*to Evenlode at the end of the week. I'll
hope to see you and Hilary here for
dinner soon.*

My love to the three of you.

> *Your affectionate aunt,*
> *Anne.*

With a sigh of satisfaction Anne Horne
folded the letter and placed it in an
envelope, which she addressed to Chief
Inspector Richard Tansey.

Other titles in the
Ulverscroft Large Print Series:

TO FIGHT THE WILD
Rod Ansell and Rachel Percy

Lost in uncharted Australian bush, Rod Ansell survived by hunting and trapping wild animals, improvising shelter and using all the bushman's skills he knew.

COROMANDEL
Pat Barr

India in the 1830s is a hot, uncomfortable place, where the East India Company still rules. Amelia and her new husband find themselves caught up in the animosities which seethe between the old order and the new.

THE SMALL PARTY
Lillian Beckwith

A frightening journey to safety begins for Ruth and her small party as their island is caught up in the dangers of armed insurrection.

FATAL RING OF LIGHT
Helen Eastwood

Katy's brother was supposed to have died in 1897 but a scrawled note in his handwriting showed July 1899. What had happened to him in those two years? Katy was determined to help him.

NIGHT ACTION
Alan Evans

Captain David Brent sails at dead of night to the German occupied Normandy town of St. Jean on a mission which will stretch loyalty and ingenuity to its limits, and beyond.

A MURDER TOO MANY
Elizabeth Ferrars

Many, including the murdered man's widow, believed the wrong man had been convicted. The further murder of a key witness in the earlier case convinced Basnett that the seemingly unrelated deaths were linked.

THE WILDERNESS WALK
Sheila Bishop

Stifling unpleasant memories of a misbegotten romance in Cleave with Lord Francis Aubrey, Lavinia goes on holiday there with her sister. The two women are thrust into a romantic intrigue involving none other than Lord Francis.

THE RELUCTANT GUEST
Rosalind Brett

Ann Calvert went to spend a month on a South African farm with Theo Borland and his sister. They both proved to be different from her first idea of them, and there was Storr Peterson — the most disturbing man she had ever met.

ONE ENCHANTED SUMMER
Anne Tedlock Brooks

A tale of mystery and romance and a girl who found both during one enchanted summer.

THE TWILIGHT MAN
Frank Gruber

Jim Rand lives alone in the California desert awaiting death. Into his hermit existence comes a teenage girl who blows both his past and his brief future wide open.

DOG IN THE DARK
Gerald Hammond

Jim Cunningham breeds and trains gun dogs, and his antagonism towards the devotees of show spaniels earns him many enemies. So when one of them is found murdered, the police are on his doorstep within hours.

THE RED KNIGHT
Geoffrey Moxon

When he finds himself a pawn on the chessboard of international espionage with his family in constant danger, Guy Trent becomes embroiled in moves and countermoves which may mean life or death for Western scientists.

CLOUD OVER MALVERTON
Nancy Buckingham

Dulcie soon realises that something is seriously wrong at Malverton, and when violence strikes she is horrified to find herself under suspicion of murder.

AFTER THOUGHTS
Max Bygraves

The Cockney entertainer tells stories of his East End childhood, of his RAF days, and his post-war showbusiness successes and friendships with fellow comedians.

MOONLIGHT
AND MARCH ROSES
D. Y. Cameron

Lynn's search to trace a missing girl takes her to Spain, where she meets Clive Hendon. While untangling the situation, she untangles her emotions and decides on her own future.

NURSE ALICE IN LOVE
Theresa Charles

Accepting the post of nurse to little Fernie Sherrod, Alice Everton could not guess at the romance, suspense and danger which lay ahead at the Sherrod's isolated estate.

POIROT INVESTIGATES
Agatha Christie

Two things bind these eleven stories together — the brilliance and uncanny skill of the diminutive Belgian detective, and the stupidity of his Watson-like partner, Captain Hastings.

LET LOOSE THE TIGERS
Josephine Cox

Queenie promised to find the long-lost son of the frail, elderly murderess, Hannah Jason. But her enquiries threatened to unlock the cage where crucial secrets had long been held captive.

TIGER TIGER
Frank Ryan

A young man involved in drugs is found murdered. This is the first event which will draw Detective Inspector Sandy Woodings into a whirlpool of murder and deceit.

CAROLINE MINUSCULE
Andrew Taylor

Caroline Minuscule, a medieval script, is the first clue to the whereabouts of a cache of diamonds. The search becomes a deadly kind of fairy story in which several murders have an other-worldly quality.

LONG CHAIN OF DEATH
Sarah Wolf

During the Second World War four American teenagers from the same town join the Army together. Forty-two years later, the son of one of the soldiers realises that someone is systematically wiping out the families of the four men.

THE LISTERDALE MYSTERY
Agatha Christie

Twelve short stories ranging from the light-hearted to the macabre, diverse mysteries ingeniously and plausibly contrived and convincingly unravelled.

TO BE LOVED
Lynne Collins

Andrew married the woman he had always loved despite the knowledge that Sarah married him for reasons of her own. So much heartache could have been avoided if only he had known how vital it was to be loved.

ACCUSED NURSE
Jane Converse

Paula found herself accused of a crime which could cost her her job, her nurse's reputation, and even the man she loved, unless the truth came to light.

BUTTERFLY MONTANE
Dorothy Cork

Parma had come to New Guinea to marry Alec Rivers, but she found him completely disinterested and that overbearing Pierce Adams getting entirely the wrong idea about her.

HONOURABLE FRIENDS
Janet Daley

Priscilla Burford is happily married when she meets Junior Environment Minister Alistair Thurston. Inevitably, sexual obsession and political necessity collide.

WANDERING MINSTRELS
Mary Delorme

Stella Wade's career as a concert pianist might have been ruined by the rudeness of a famous conductor, so it seemed to her agent and benefactor. Even Sir Nicholas fails to see the possibilities when John Tallis falls deeply in love with Stella.

CHATEAU OF FLOWERS
Margaret Rome

Alain, Comte de Treville needed a wife to look after him, and Fleur went into marriage on a business basis only, hoping that eventually he would come to trust and care for her.

CRISS-CROSS
Alan Scholefield

As her ex-husband had succeeded in kidnapping their young daughter once, Jane was determined to take her safely back to England. But all too soon Jane is caught up in a new web of intrigue.

DEAD BY MORNING
Dorothy Simpson

Leo Martindale's body was discovered outside the gates of his ancestral home. Is it, as Inspector Thanet begins to suspect, murder?